STINKY

What's that?
DINOS!

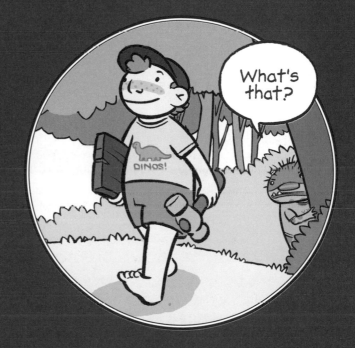

A TOON BOOK BY

ELEANOR DAVIS

TOON BOOKS, A DIVISION OF RAW JUNIOR, LLC, NEW YORK

WWW.TOON-BOOKS.COM

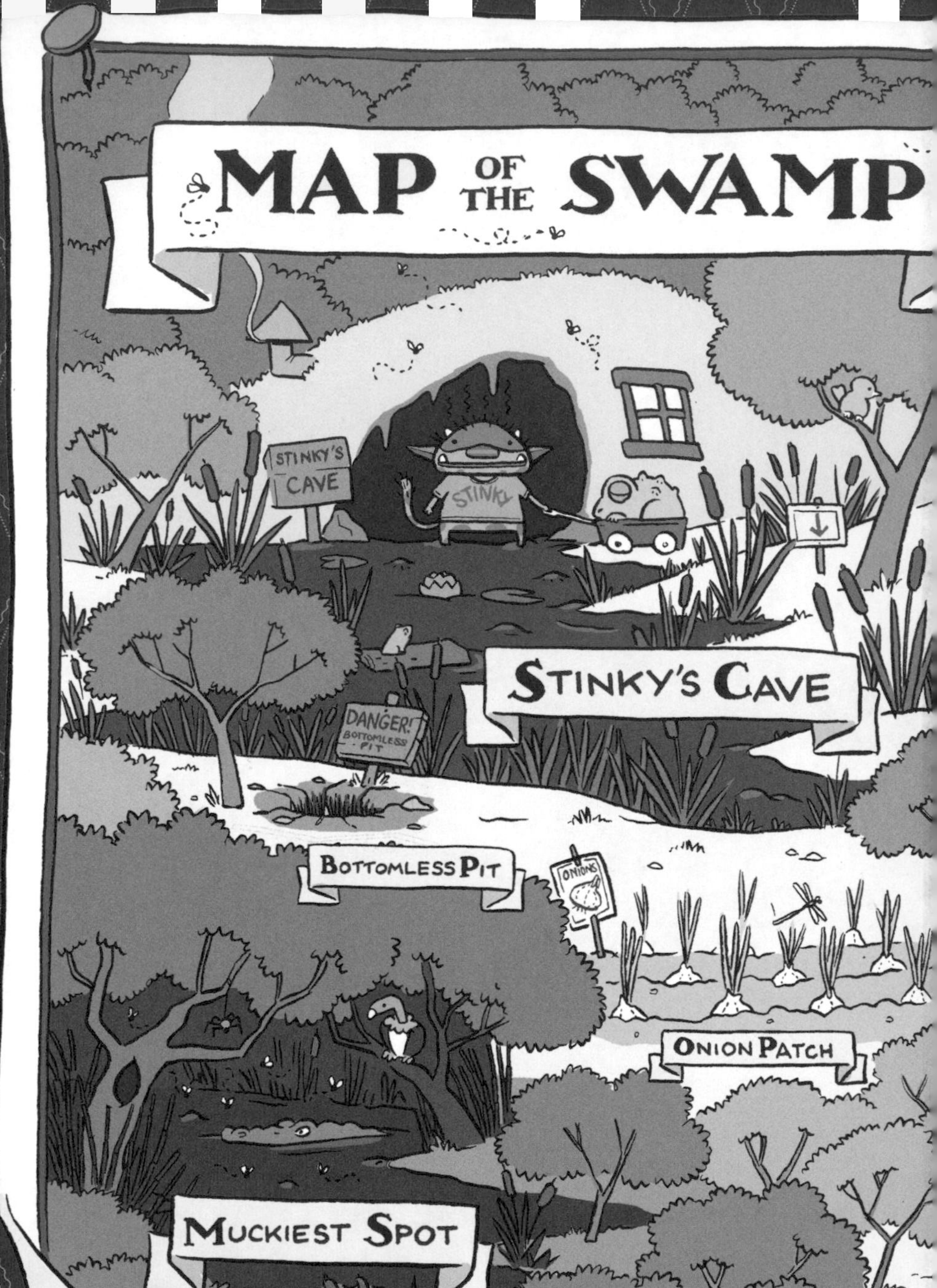
MAP OF THE SWAMP
STINKY'S CAVE
STINKY
STINKY'S CAVE
DANGER! BOTTOMLESS PIT
BOTTOMLESS PIT
ONIONS
ONION PATCH
MUCKIEST SPOT

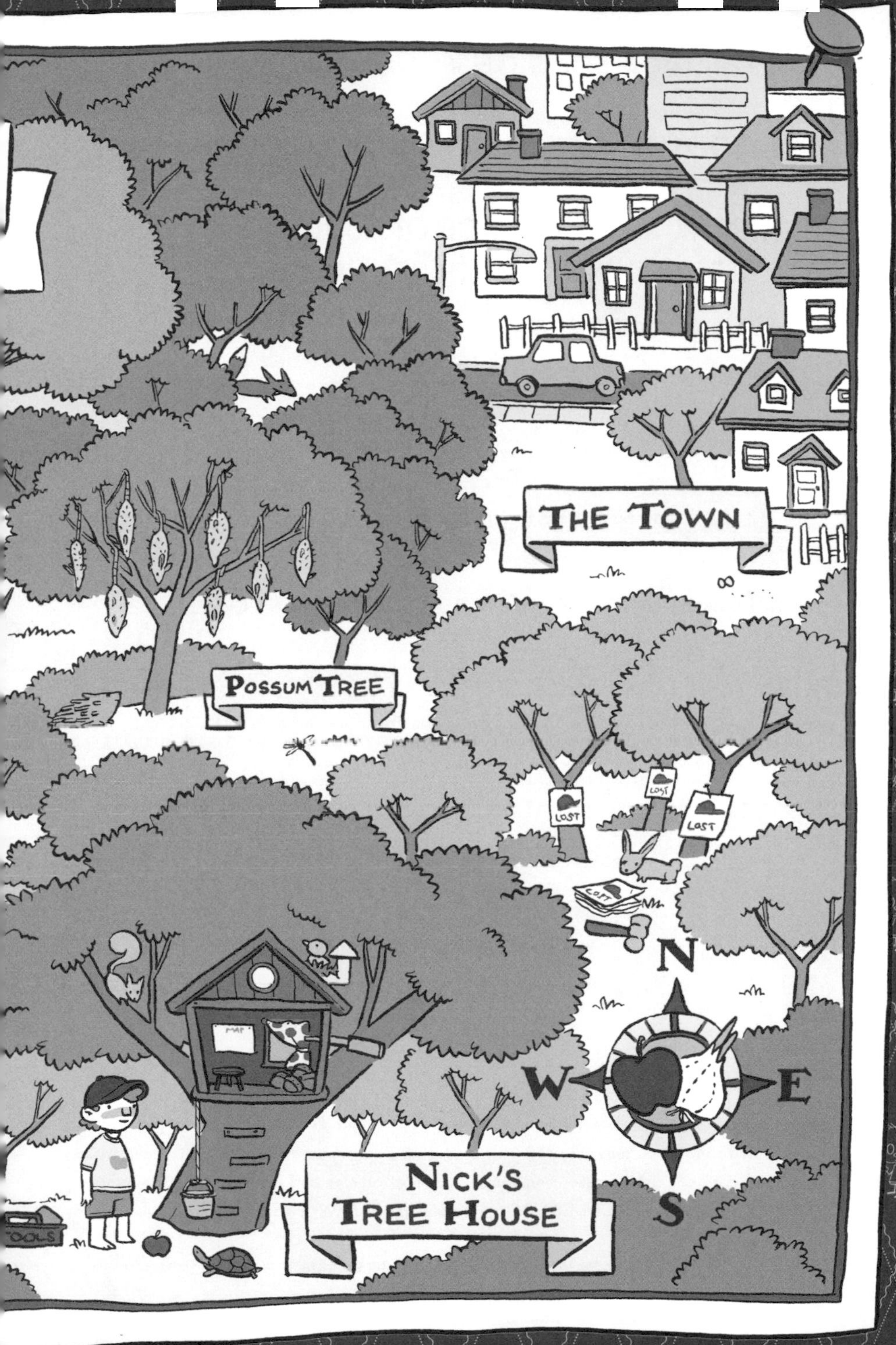
THE TOWN
POSSUM TREE
LOST
LOST
LOST
N
W
E
S
MAP
NICK'S
TREE HOUSE

A THEODOR SEUSS GEISEL HONOR BOOK

A BOOKLIST NOTABLE CHILDREN'S BOOK

A BANK STREET COLLEGE OF EDUCATION BEST CHILDREN'S BOOK OF THE YEAR

A TOON BOOK

Editorial Director: FRANÇOISE MOULY
Advisor: ART SPIEGELMAN

Book Design: FRANÇOISE MOULY & JONATHAN BENNETT

 Library of Congress Control Number: 2007943857

ISBN 13: 978-1-935179-06-1 ISBN 10: 1-935179-06-3
Paperback edition
10 9 8 7 6 5 4 3 2 1

www.TOON-BOOKS.com

CHAPTER ONE

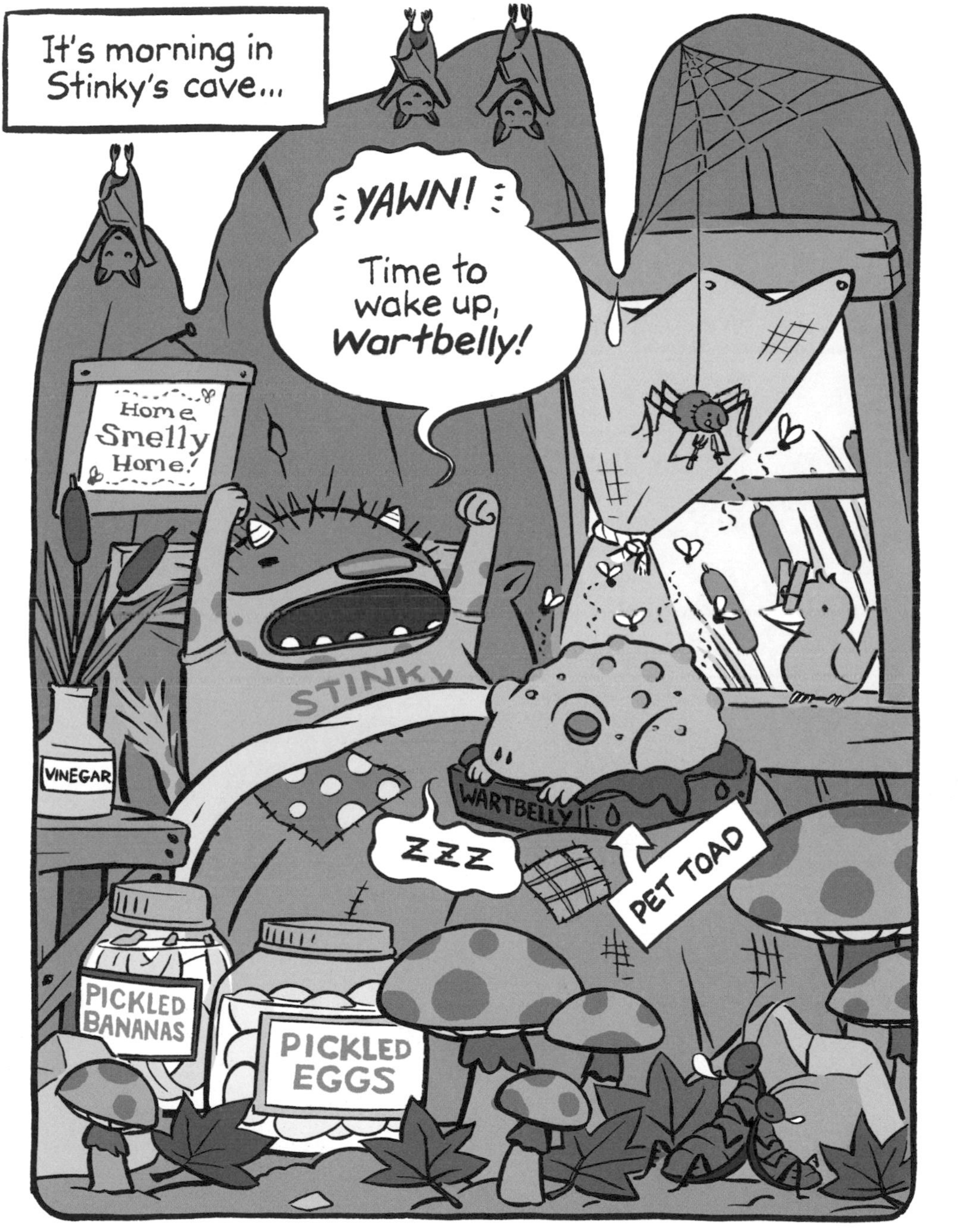
It's morning in Stinky's cave...
YAWN!
Time to wake up, Wartbelly!
Home Smelly Home!
VINEGAR
STINKY
WARTBELLY
ZZZ
PET TOAD
PICKLED BANANAS
PICKLED EGGS

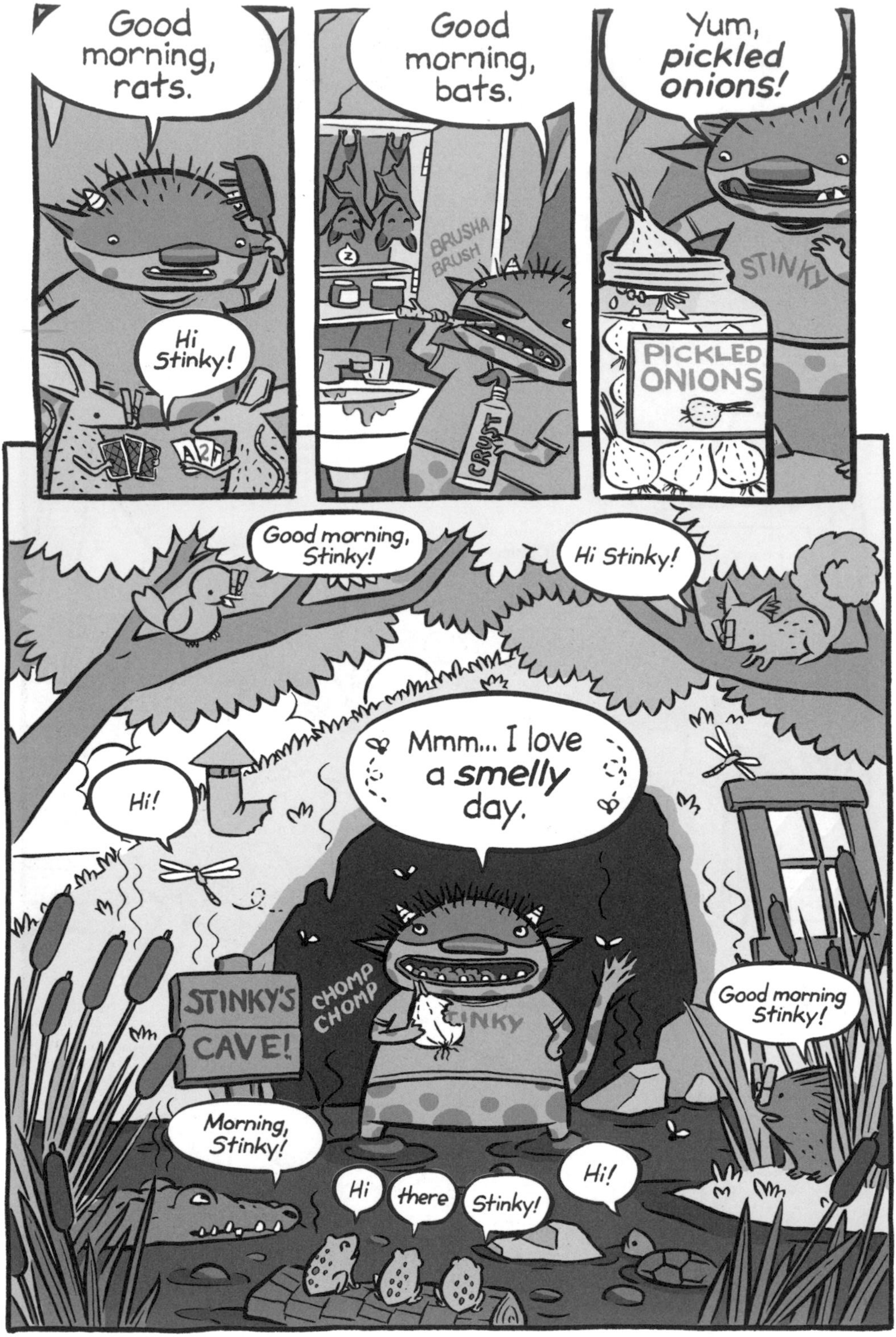
Good morning, rats.
Hi Stinky!
Good morning, bats.
BRUSHA BRUSH
CRUST
Yum, pickled onions!
PICKLED ONIONS
STINKY
Good morning, Stinky!
Hi Stinky!
Hi!
Mmm... I love a smelly day.
STINKY'S CAVE!
CHOMP CHOMP
STINKY
Good morning Stinky!
Morning, Stinky!
Hi
there
Stinky!
Hi!

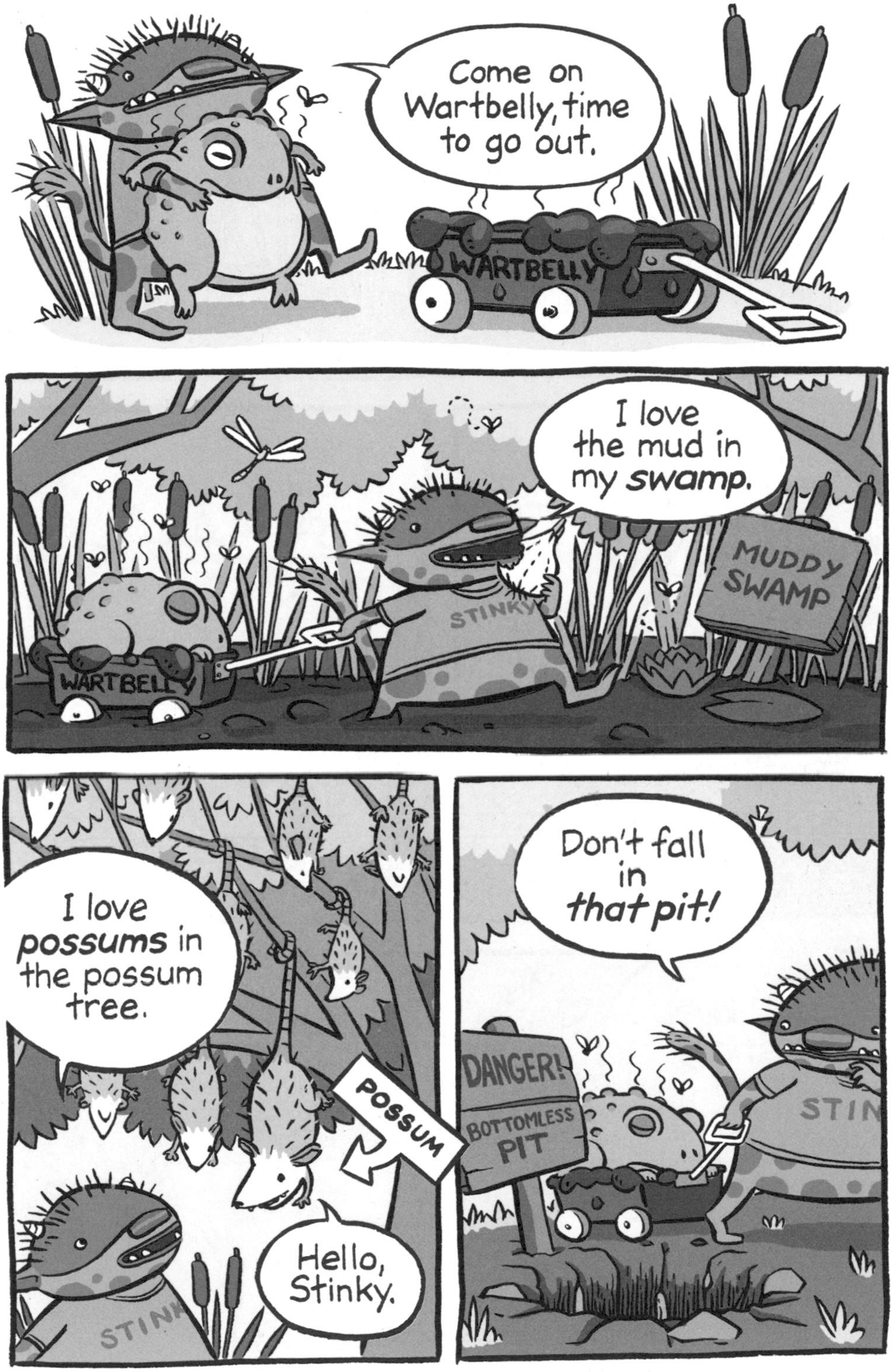
Come on Wartbelly, time to go out.
WARTBELLY
I love the mud in my *swamp.*
WARTBELLY
STINKY
MUDDY SWAMP
I love **possums** in the possum tree.
POSSUM
Hello, Stinky.
Don't fall in *that pit!*
DANGER!
BOTTOMLESS PIT

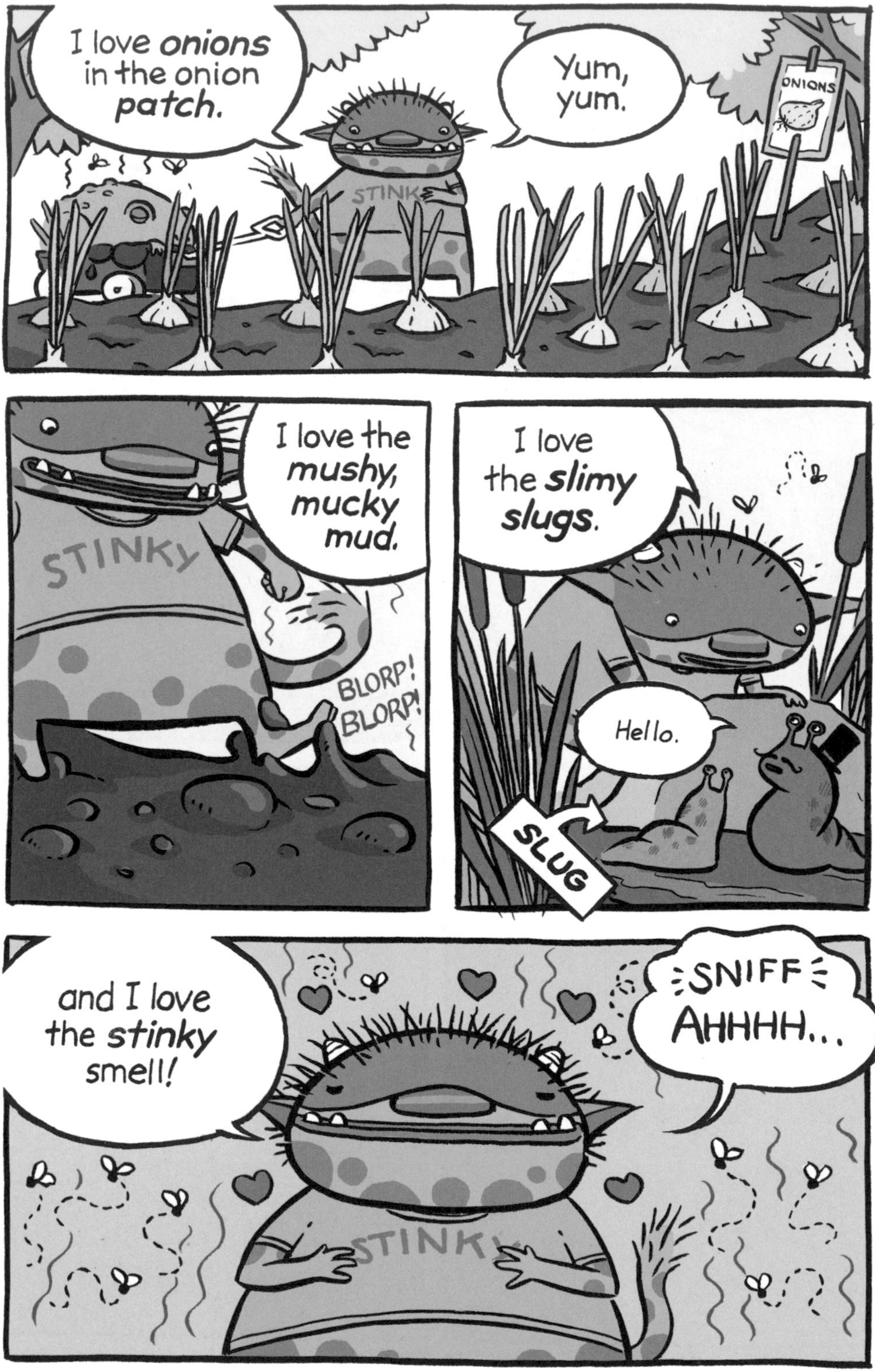
I love onions in the onion patch.
Yum, yum.
ONIONS
STINKY
I love the mushy, mucky mud.
STINKY
BLORP! BLORP!
I love the slimy slugs.
Hello.
SLUG
and I love the stinky smell!
SNIFF
AHHHH...
STINKY

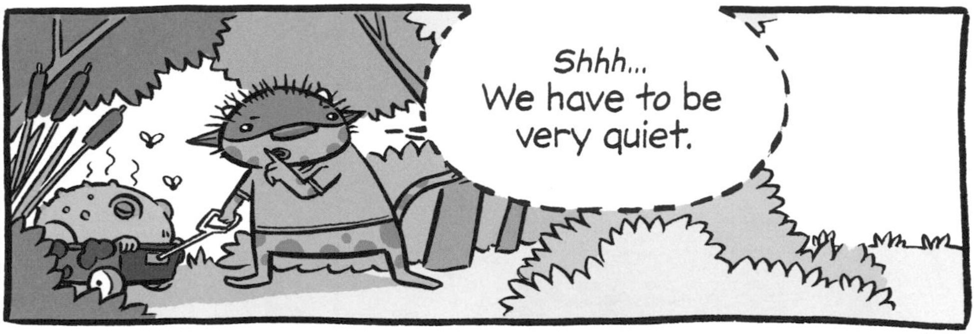
Shhh...
We have to be very quiet.

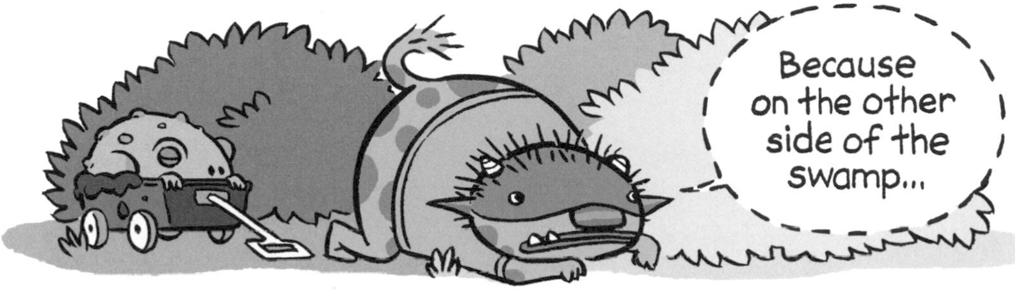
Because on the other side of the swamp...

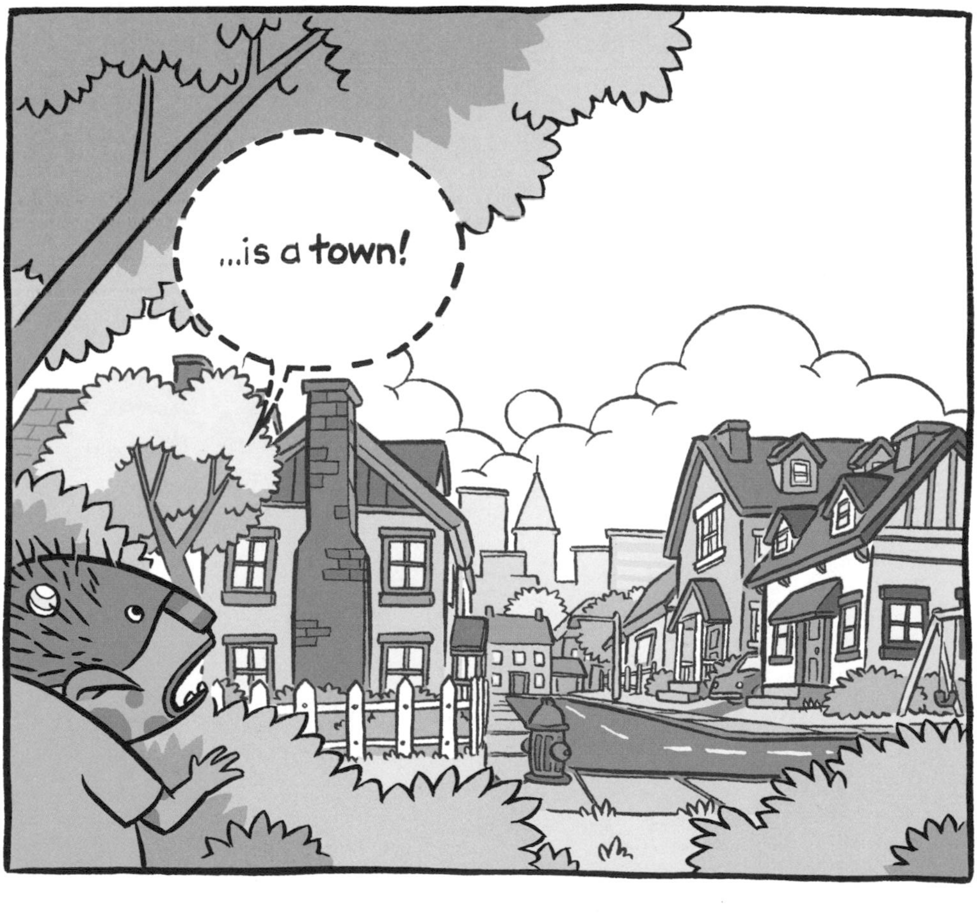
...is a **town!**

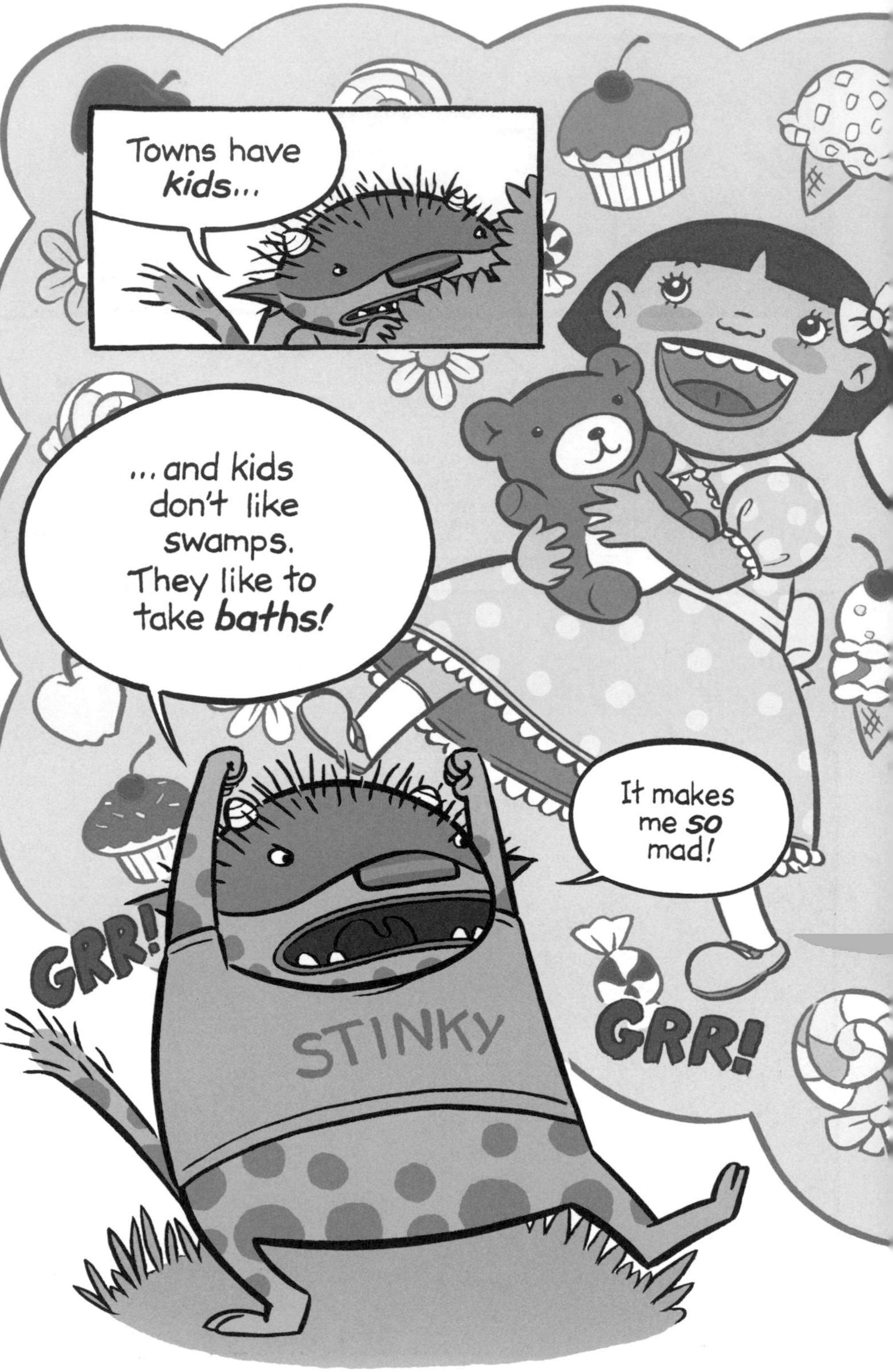
Towns have kids...
... and kids don't like swamps. They like to take baths!
It makes me so mad!
GRR!
STINKY
GRR!

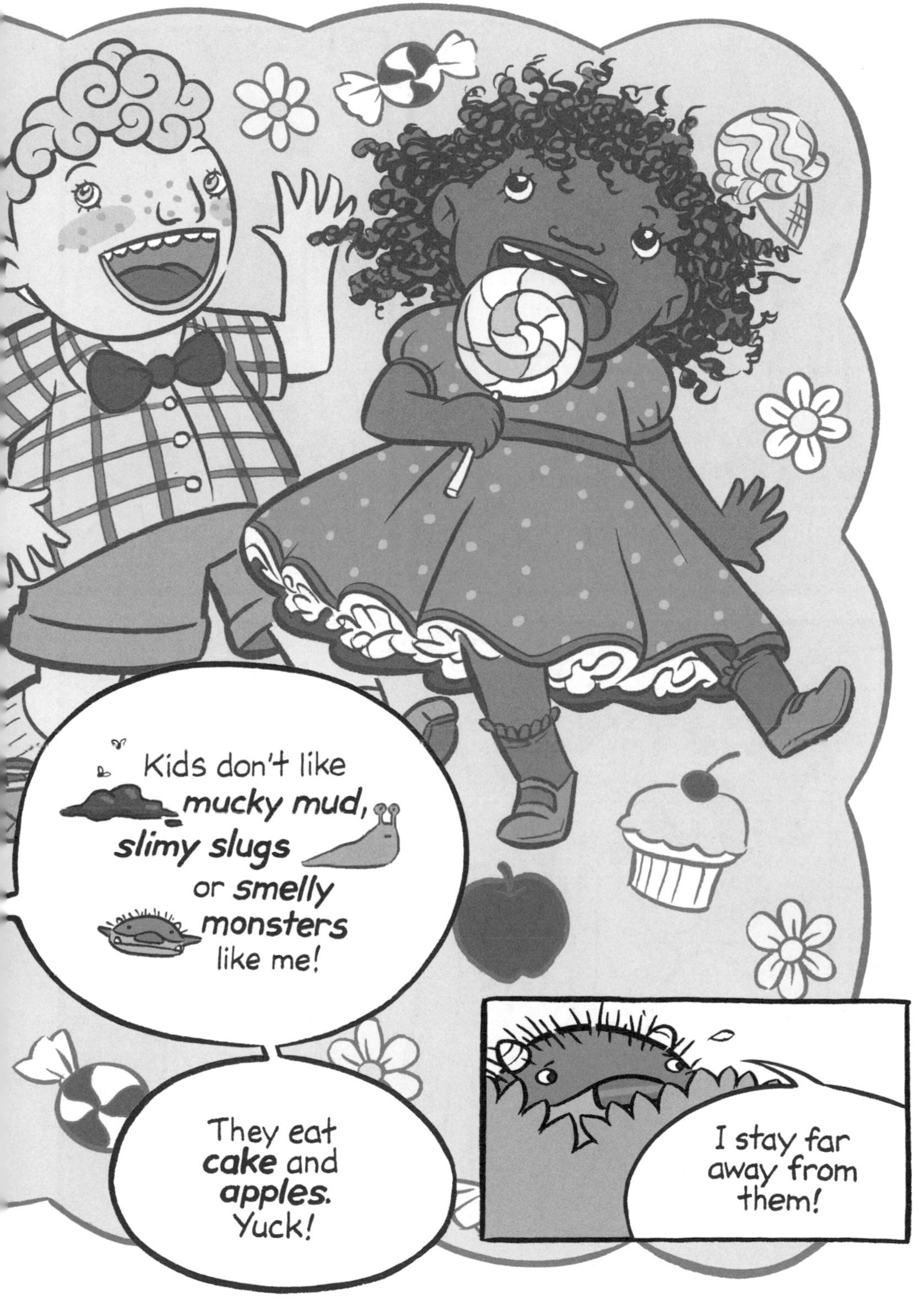
Kids don't like mucky mud, slimy slugs or smelly monsters like me!
They eat cake and apples. Yuck!
I stay far away from them!

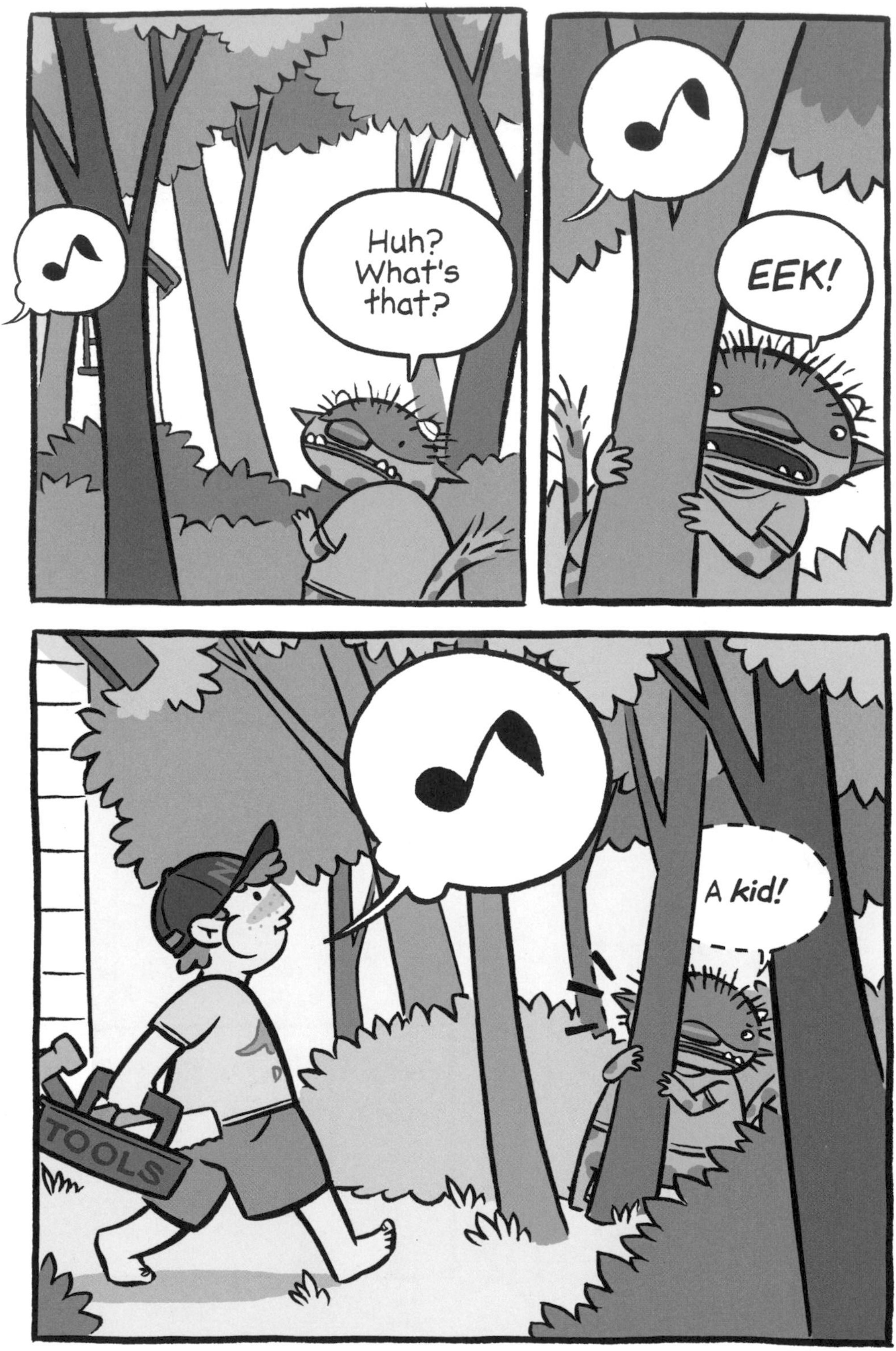
♪
Huh? What's that?
♪
EEK!
♪
A kid!
TOOLS

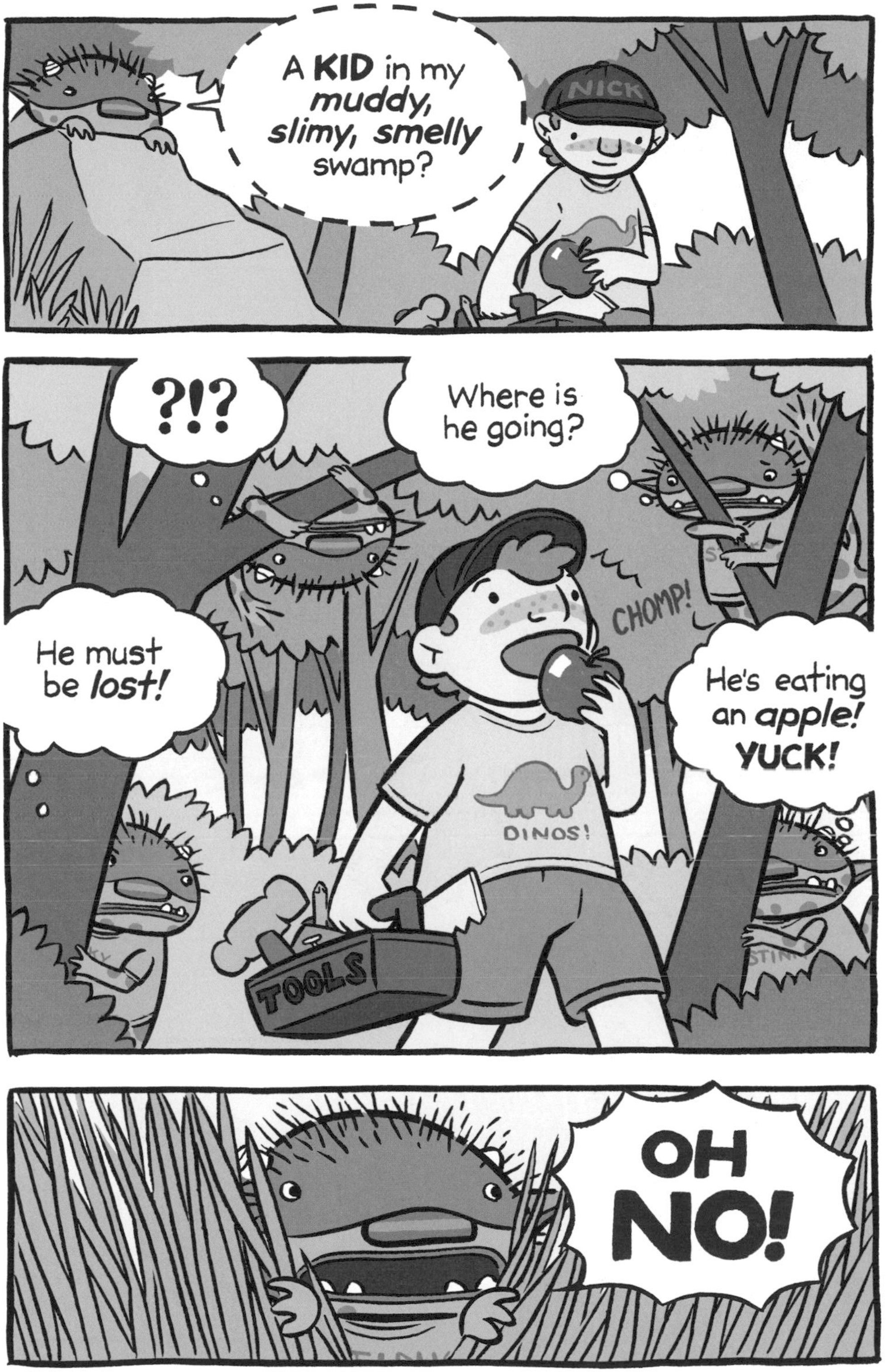
A **KID** in my *muddy, slimy, smelly* swamp?
NICK
?!?
Where is he going?
CHOMP!
He must be *lost!*
He's eating an *apple!* **YUCK!**
DINOS!
TOOLS
OH NO!

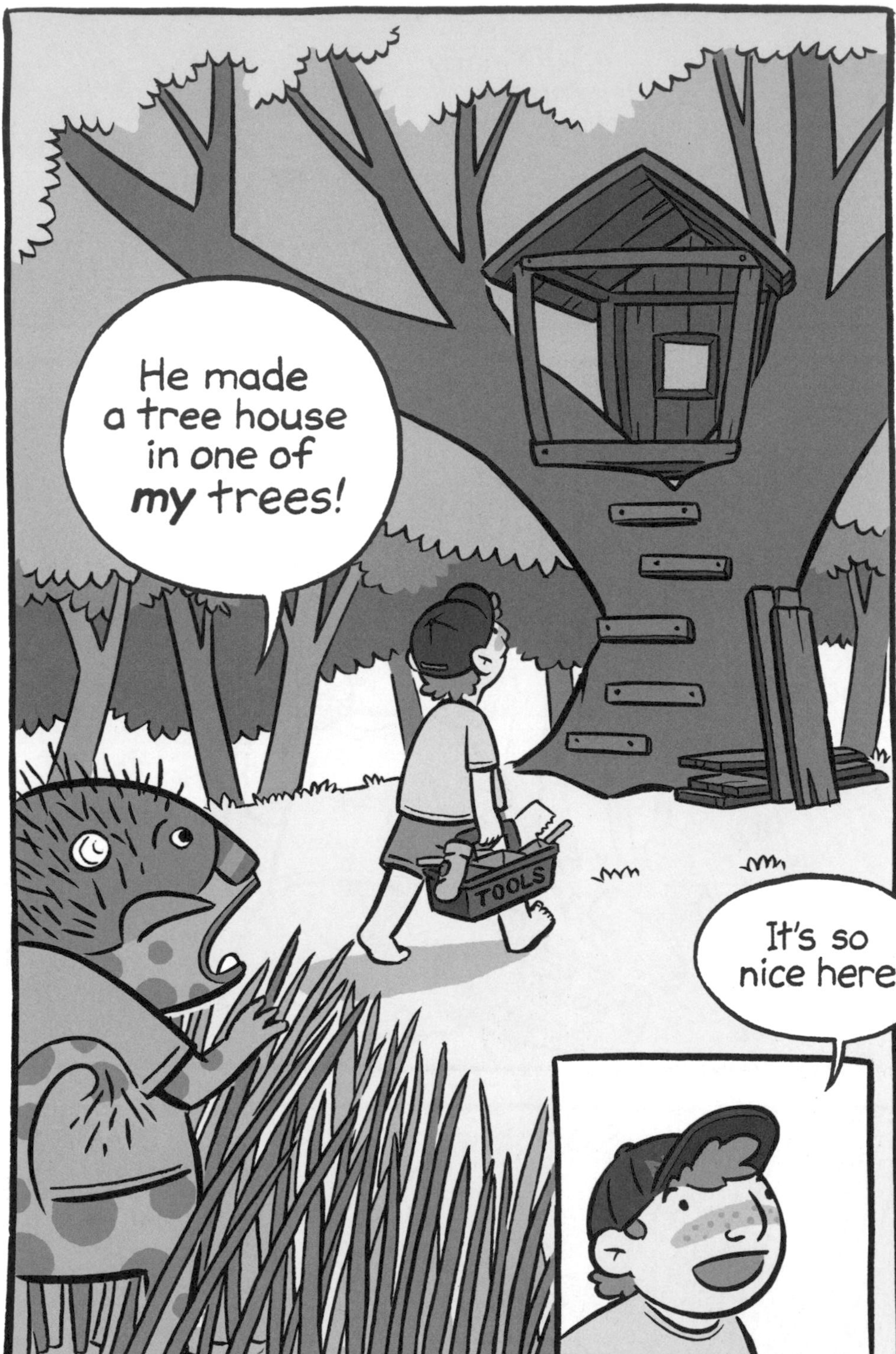
He made a tree house in one of **my** trees!
TOOLS
It's so nice here!

CHAPTER TWO

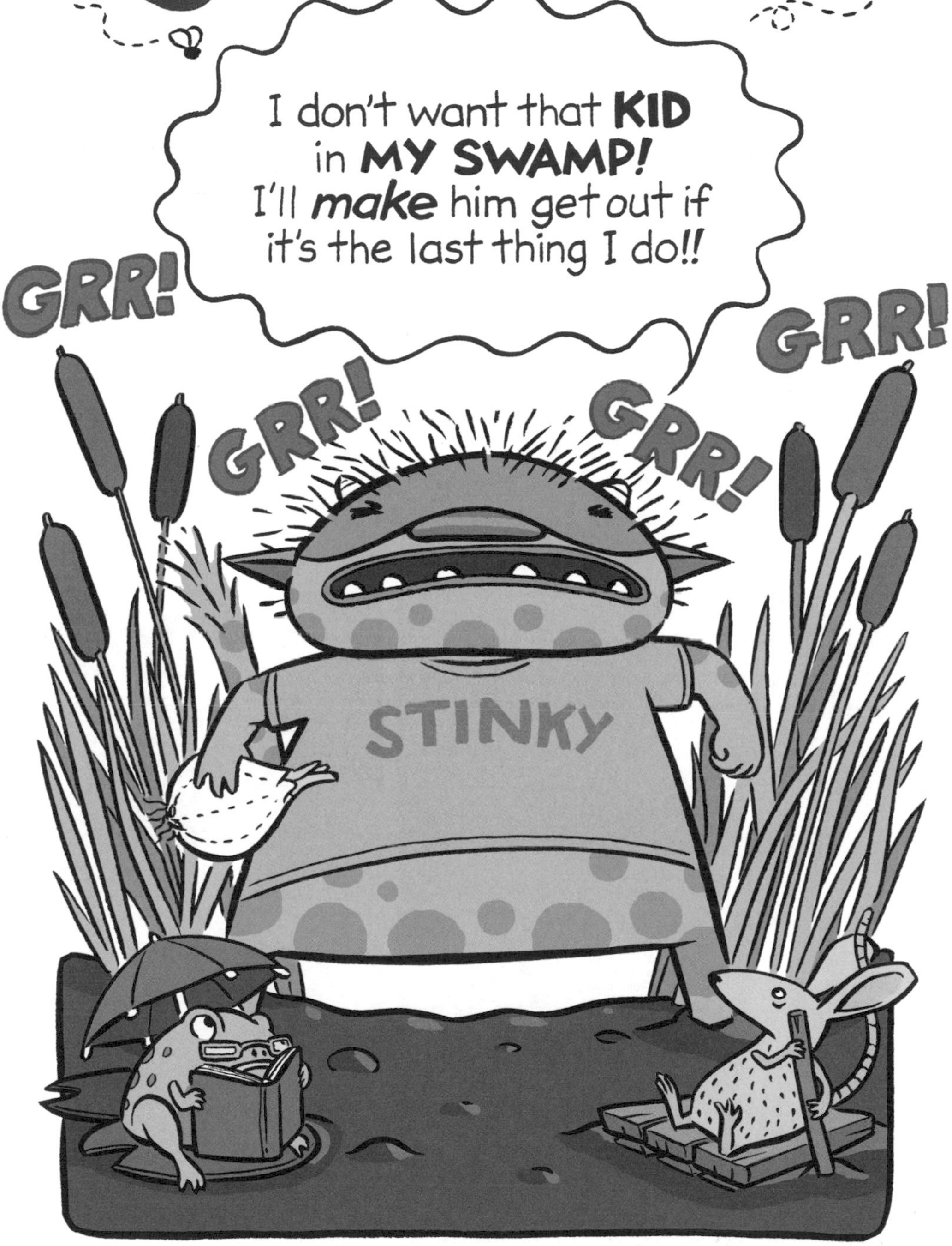
I don't want that **KID** in **MY SWAMP!** I'll *make* him get out if it's the last thing I do!!
GRR!
GRR!
GRR!
GRR!
STINKY

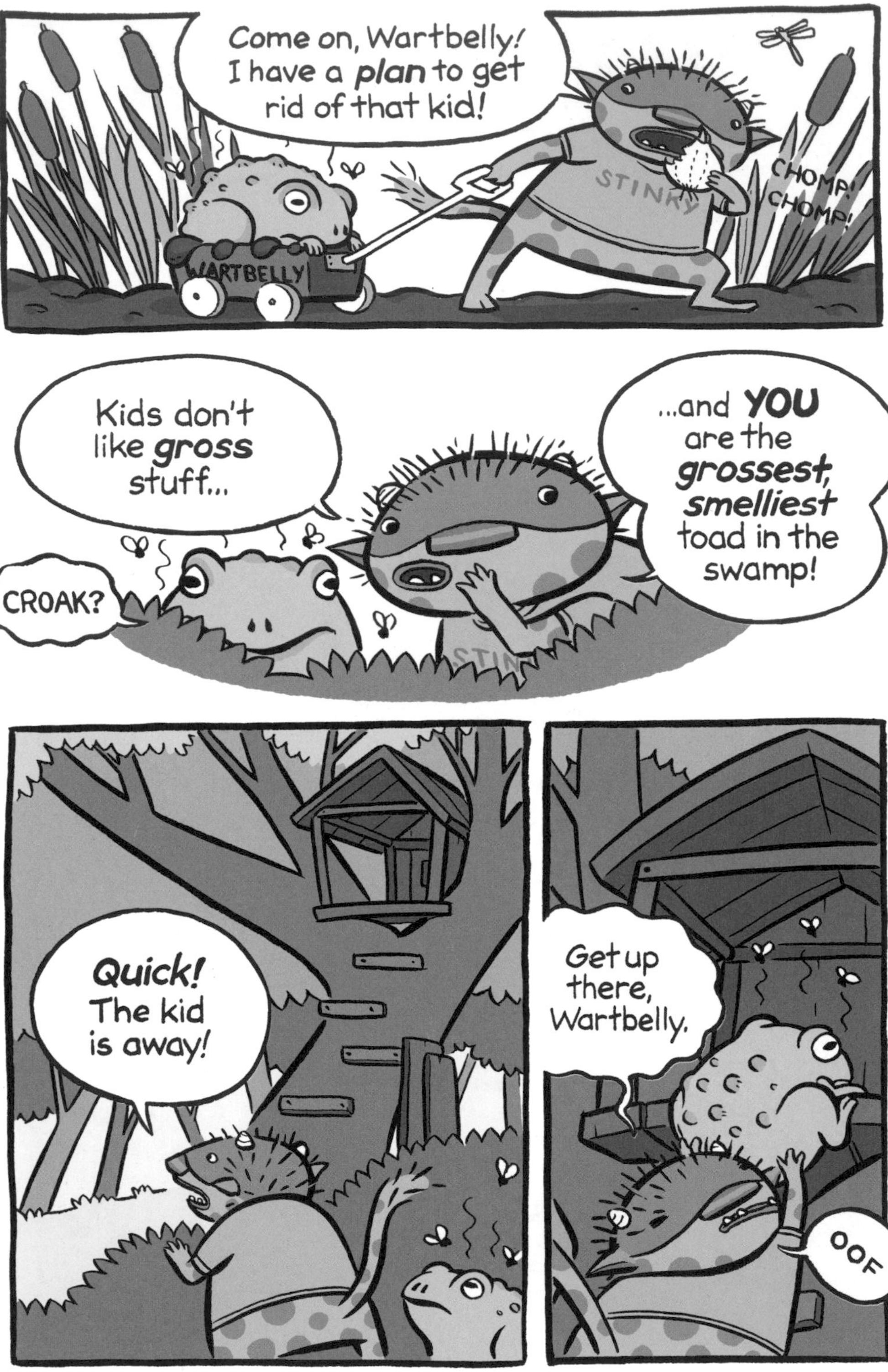
Come on, Wartbelly! I have a **plan** to get rid of that kid!
WARTBELLY
STINKY
CHOMP! CHOMP!
Kids don't like **gross** stuff...
...and **YOU** are the **grossest, smelliest** toad in the swamp!
CROAK?
Quick! The kid is away!
Get up there, Wartbelly.
OOF

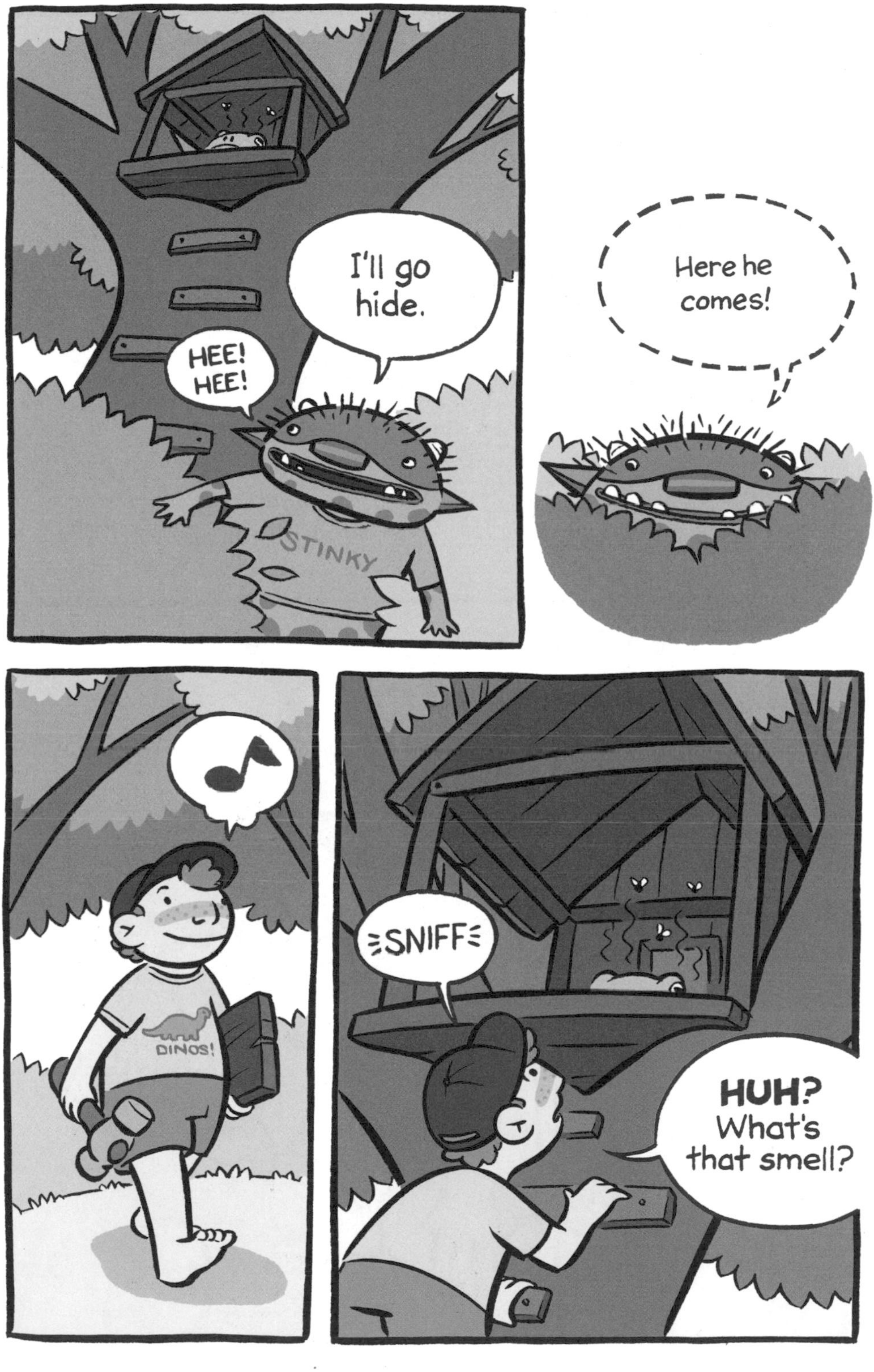
HEE!
HEE!
I'll go hide.
STINKY
Here he comes!
DINOS!
SNIFF
HUH?
What's that smell?

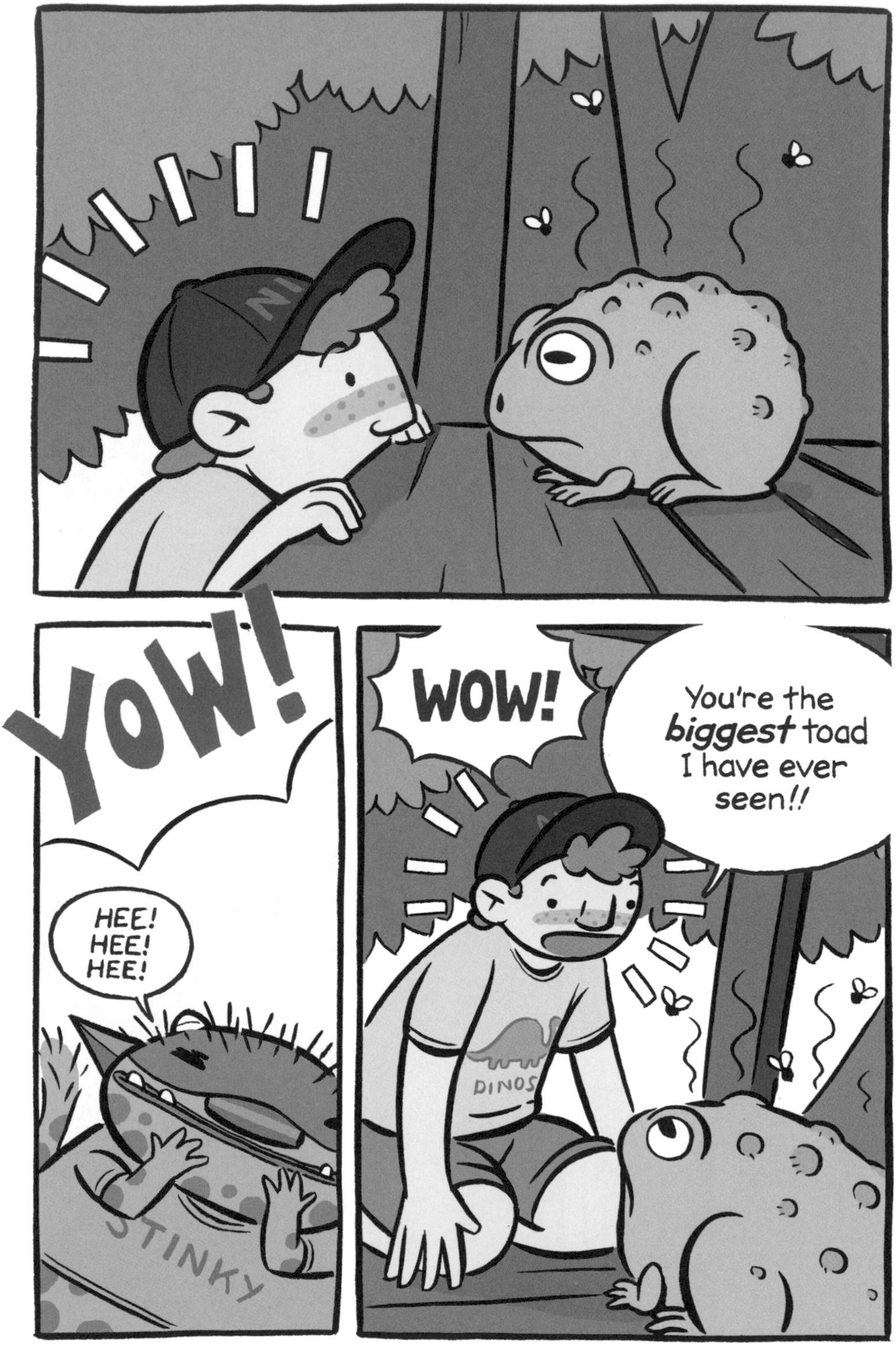
YOW!
HEE! HEE! HEE!
STINKY
WOW!
You're the *biggest* toad I have ever seen!!
DINOS

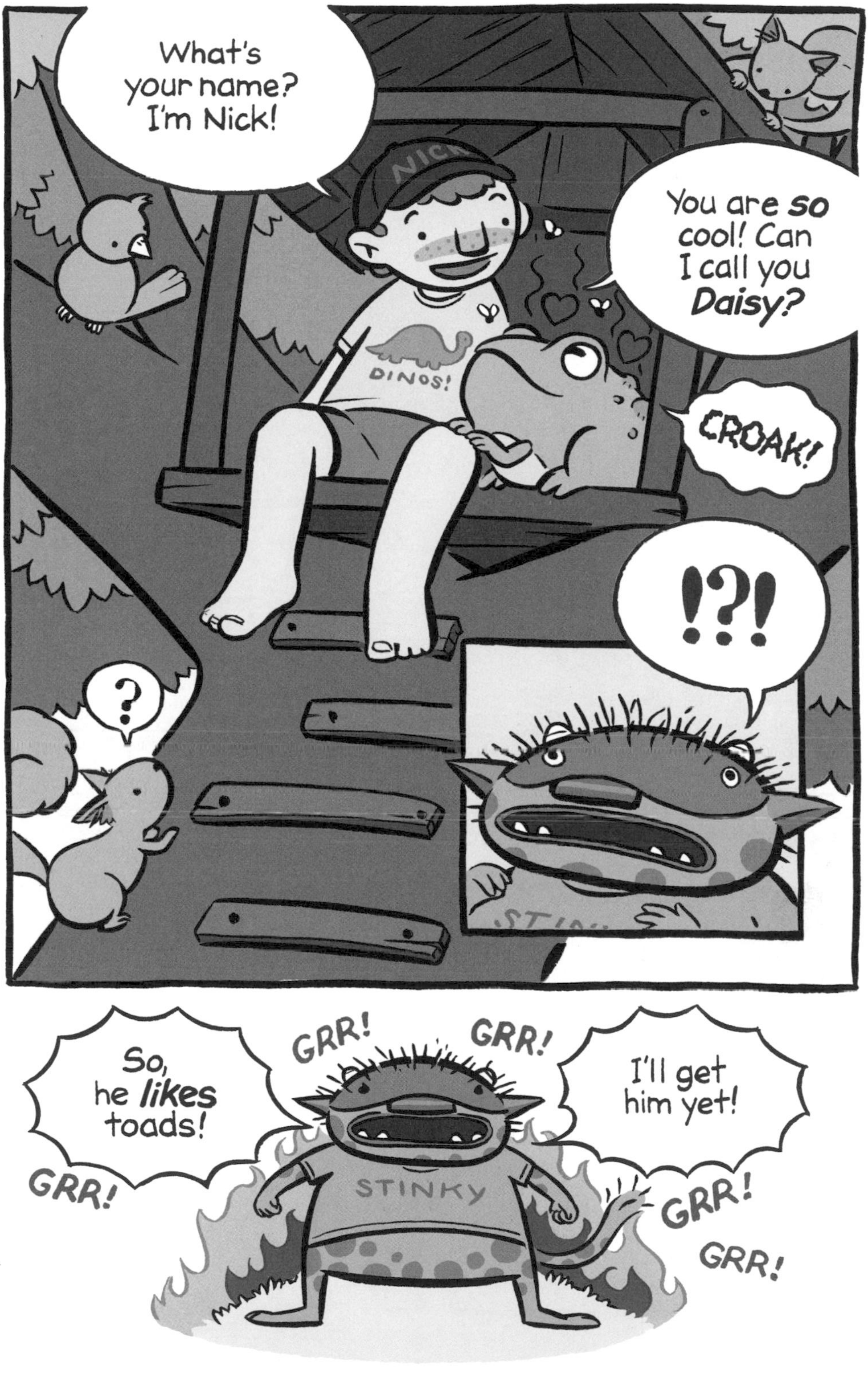
What's your name? I'm Nick!
NICK
You are **so** cool! Can I call you ***Daisy?***
DINOS!
CROAK!
?
!?!
So, he ***likes*** toads!
GRR!
GRR!
I'll get him yet!
STINKY
GRR!
GRR!
GRR!

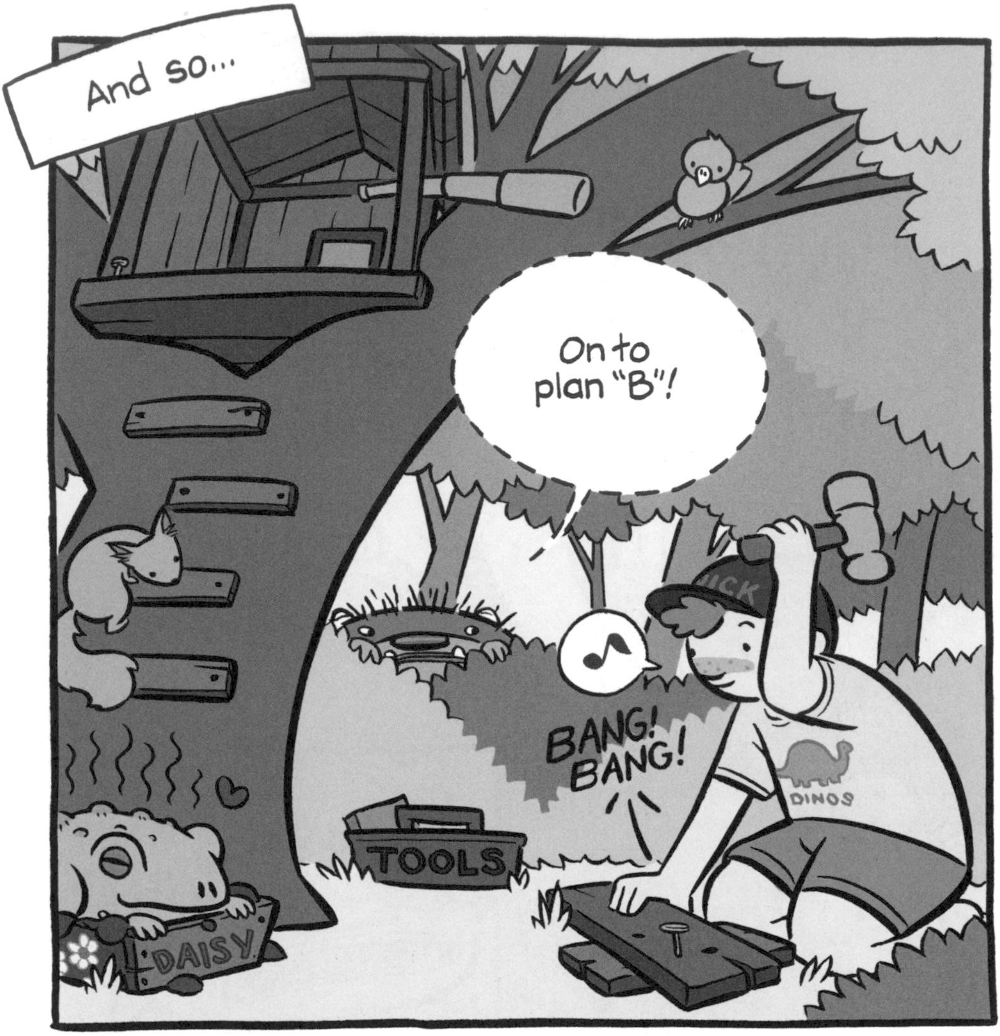
And so...
On to plan "B"!
BANG! BANG!
TOOLS
DAISY
DINOS

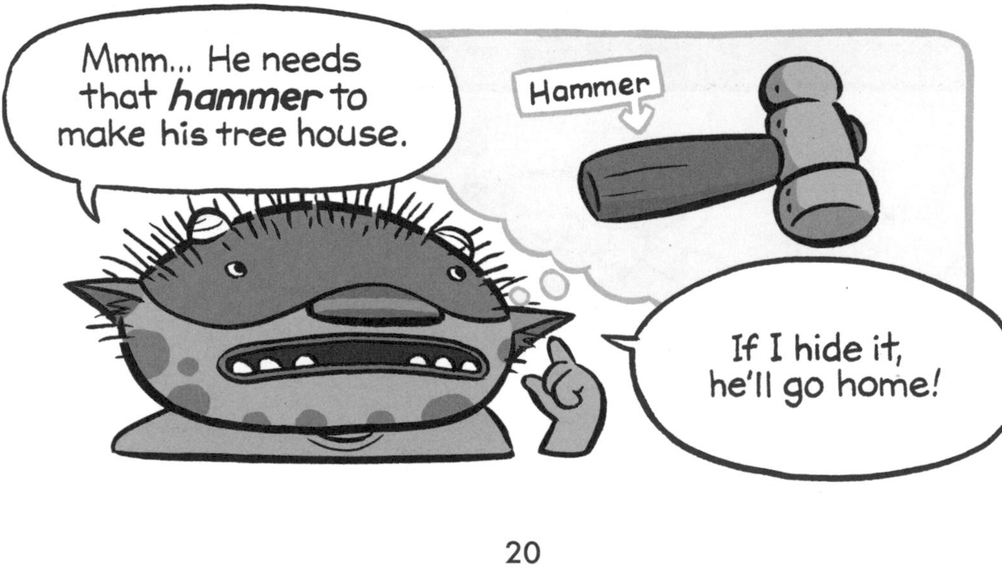
Mmm... He needs that **hammer** to make his tree house.
Hammer
If I hide it, he'll go home!

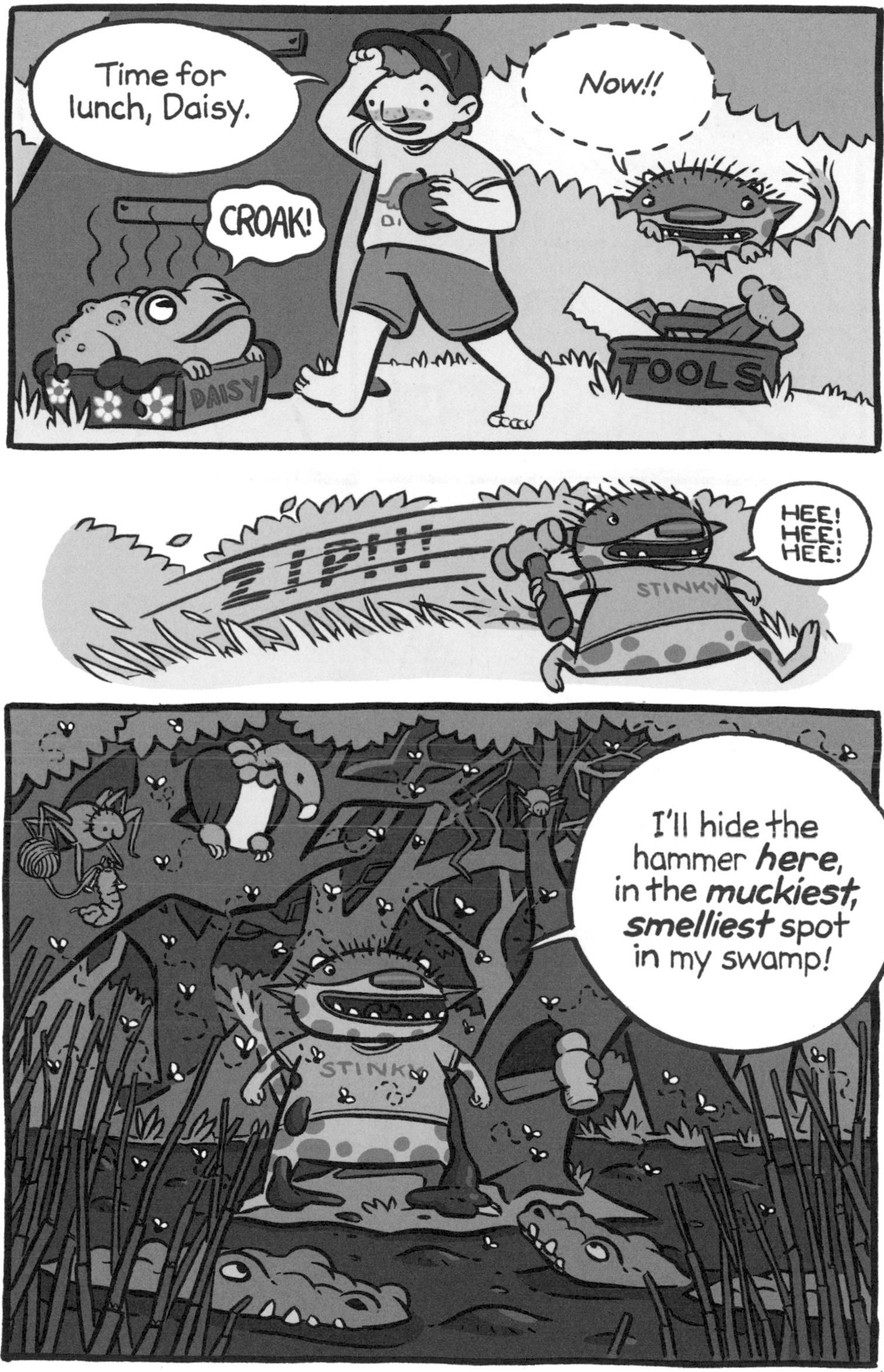
Time for lunch, Daisy.
Now!!
CROAK!
DI
DAISY
TOOLS
ZIP!!!
HEE! HEE! HEE!
STINKY
I'll hide the hammer ***here***, in the ***muckiest, smelliest*** spot in my swamp!
STINKY

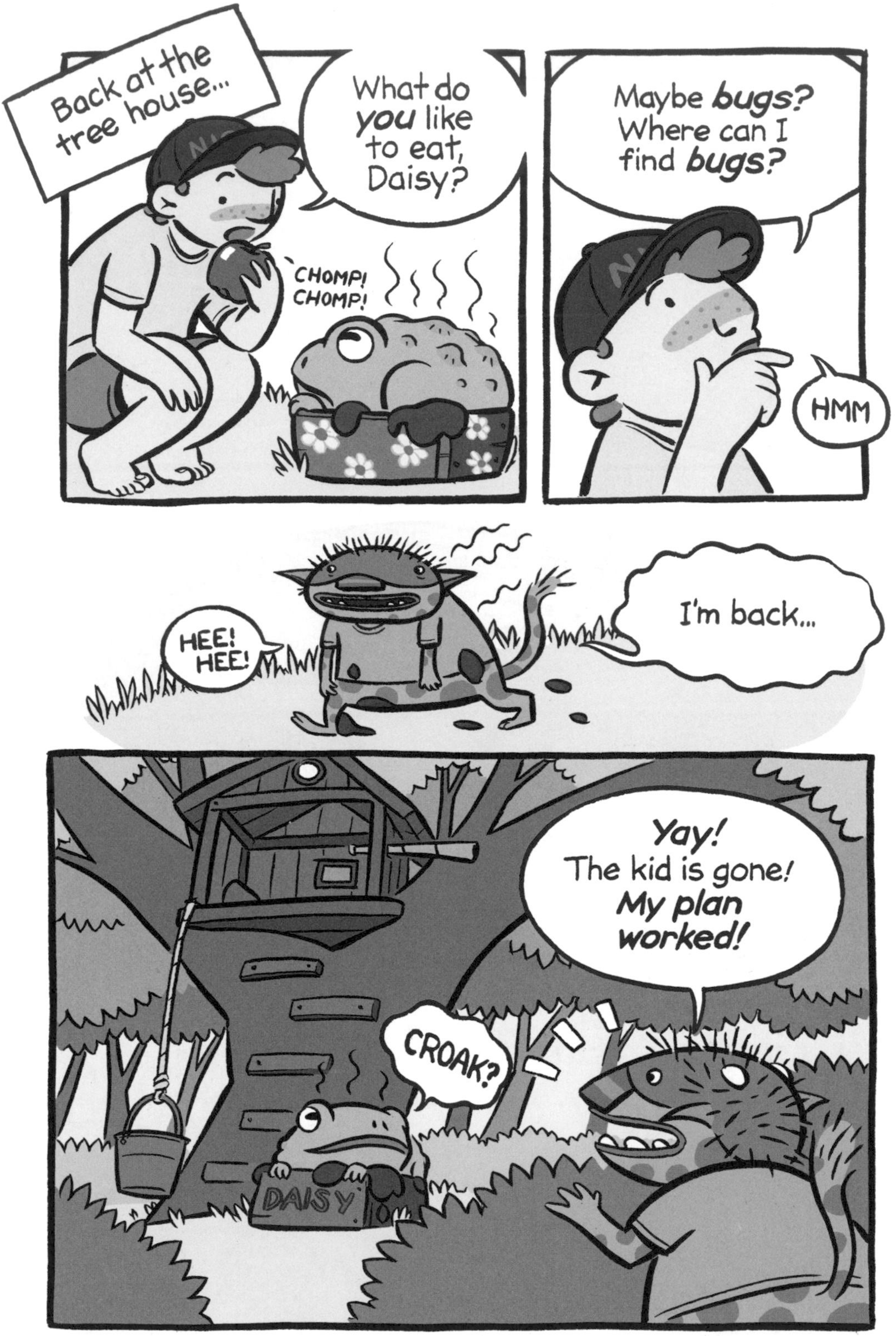

Back at the tree house...
What do *you* like to eat, Daisy?
CHOMP! CHOMP!
Maybe *bugs?* Where can I find *bugs?*
HMM
HEE! HEE!
I'm back...
Yay! The kid is gone! *My plan worked!*
CROAK?
DAISY

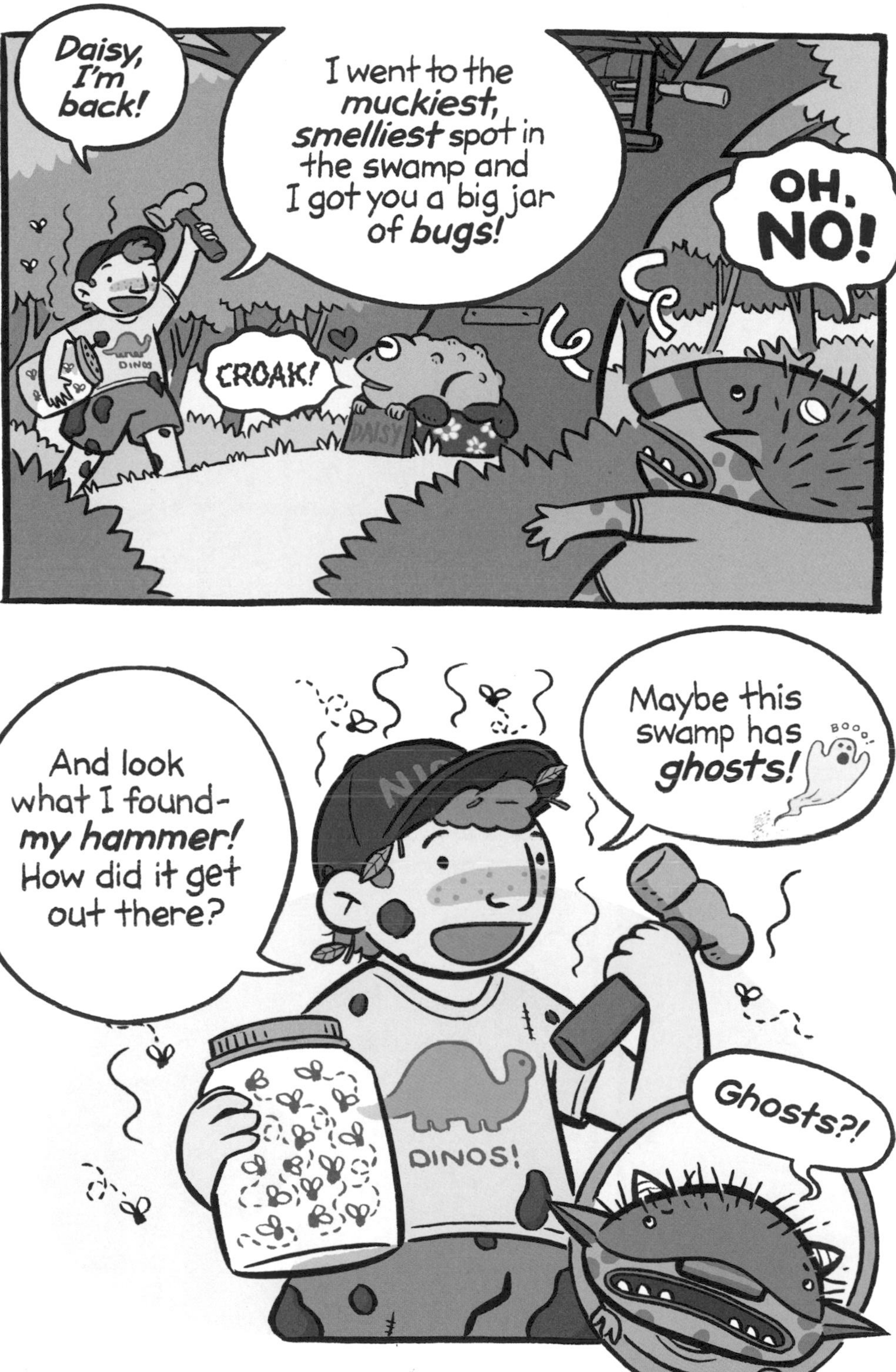
Daisy, I'm back!
I went to the muckiest, smelliest spot in the swamp and I got you a big jar of bugs!
OH, NO!
CROAK!
DINOS
DAISY
And look what I found- my hammer! How did it get out there?
Maybe this swamp has ghosts!
BOOO..
DINOS!
Ghosts?!

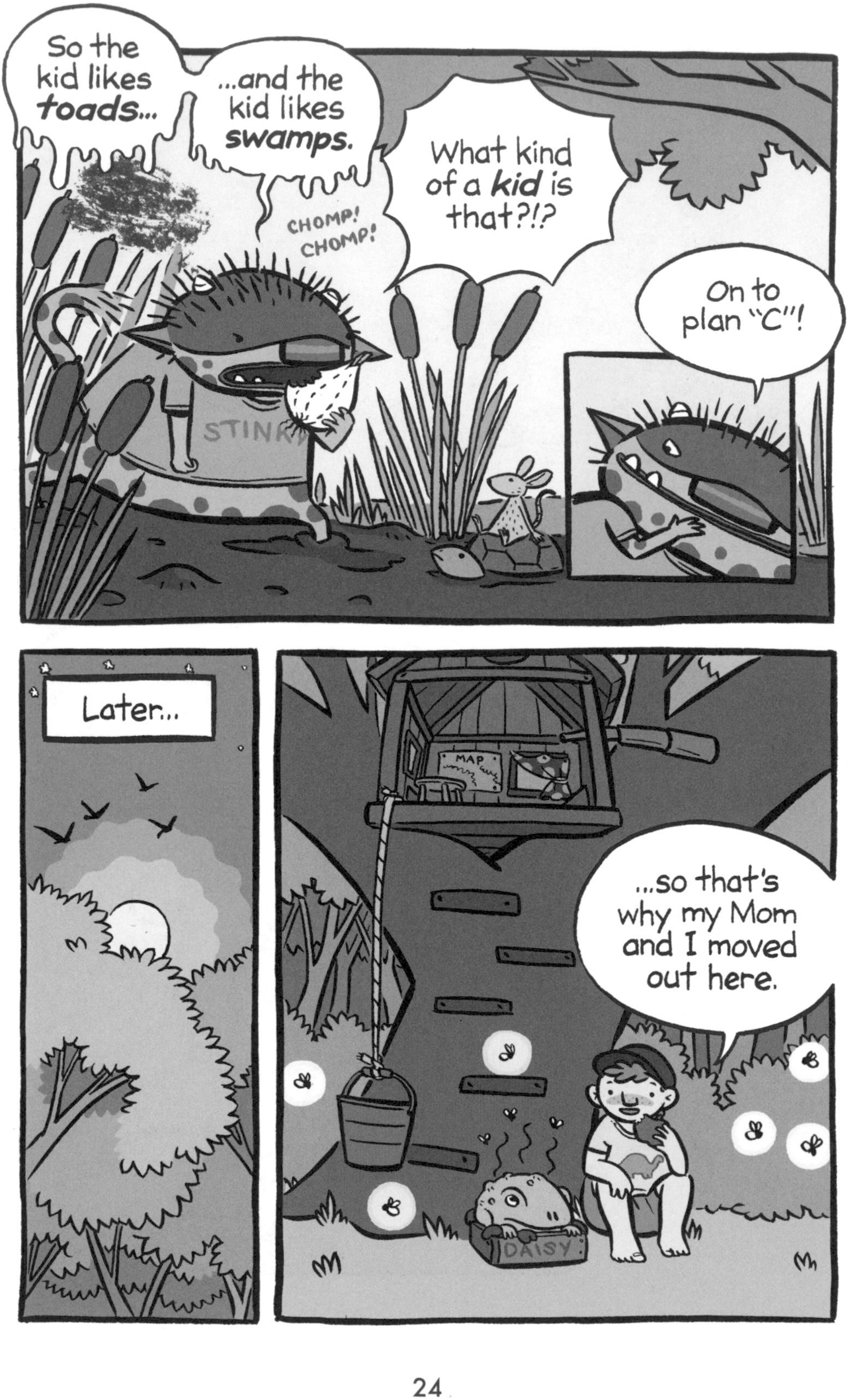
So the kid likes **toads**...
...and the kid likes **swamps**.
CHOMP! CHOMP!
What kind of a **kid** is that?!?
STINKY
On to plan "C"!
Later...
MAP
...so that's why my Mom and I moved out here.
DAISY

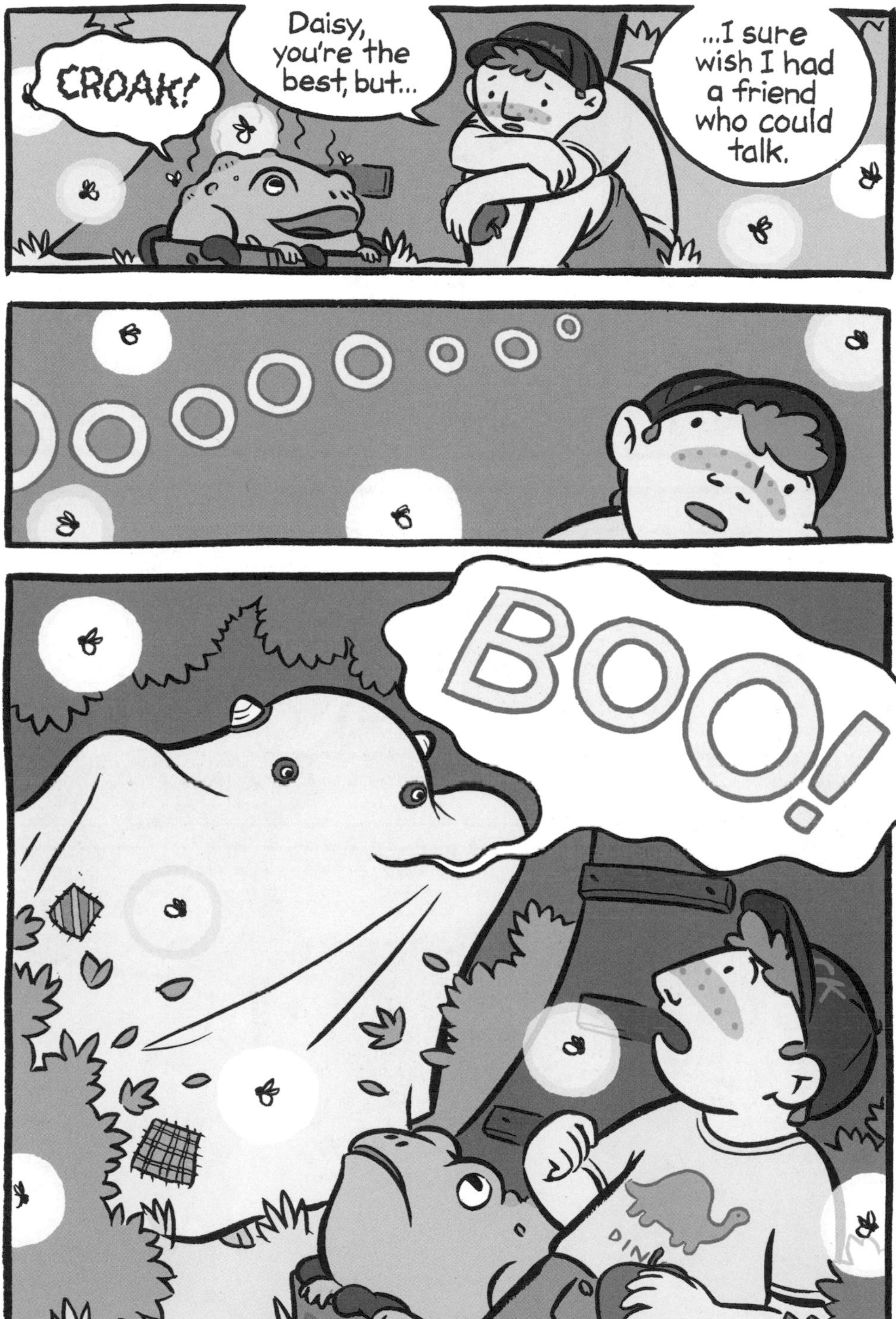
CROAK!
Daisy, you're the best, but...
...I sure wish I had a friend who could talk.
BOO!
DAISY

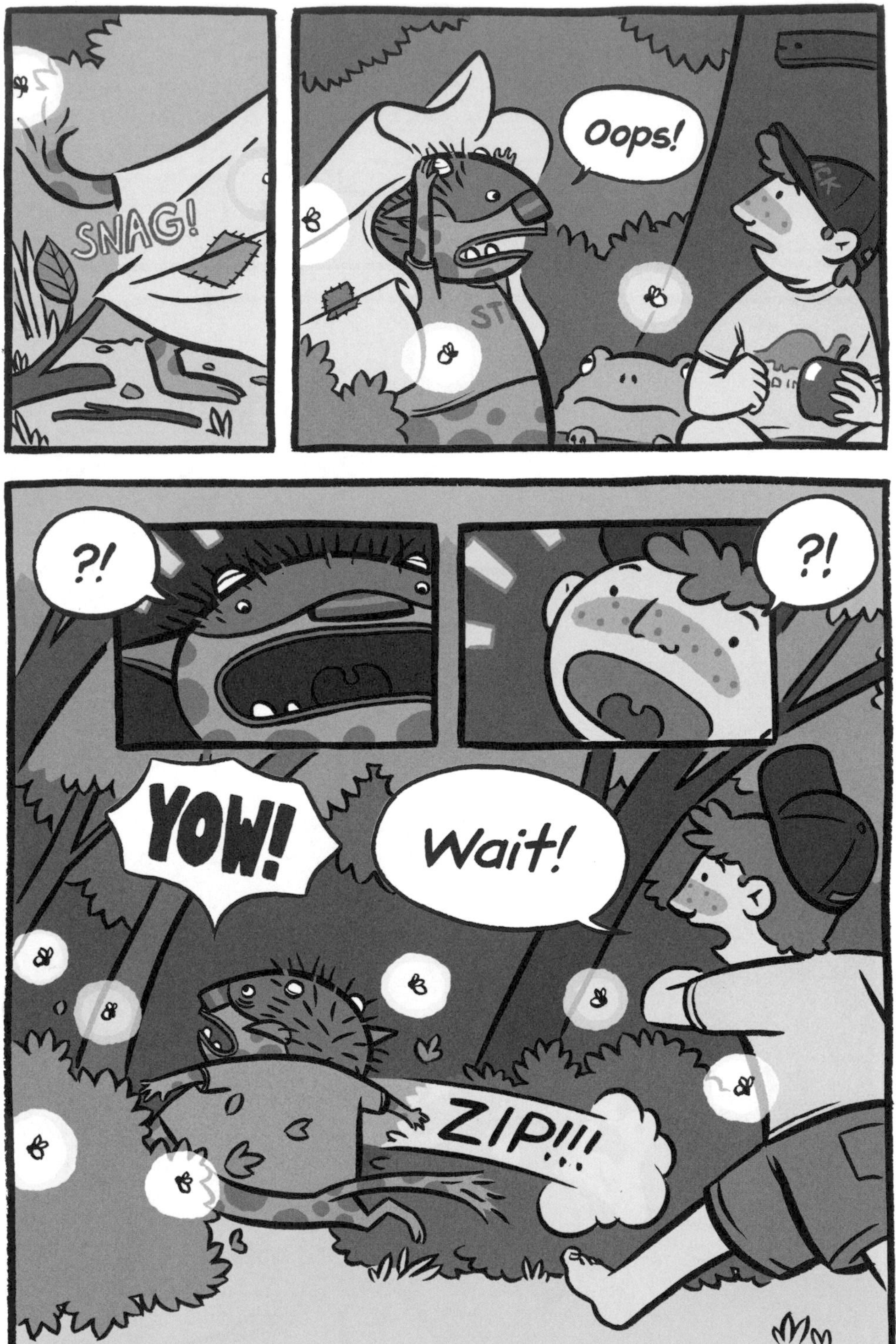
SNAG!
Oops!
?!
?!
YOW!
Wait!
ZIP!!!

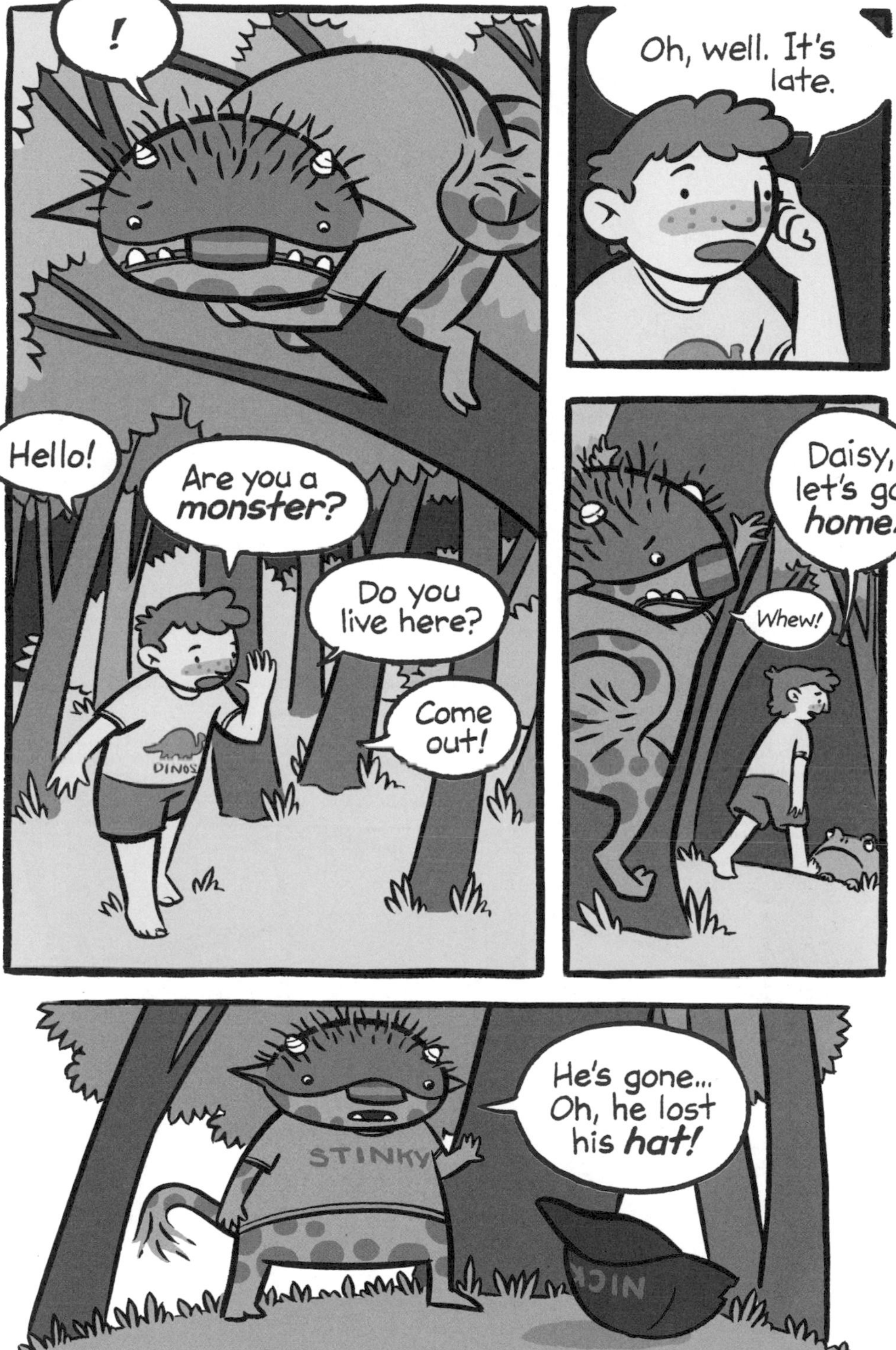
!
Hello!
Are you a monster?
Do you live here?
Come out!
Oh, well. It's late.
Daisy, let's go home.
Whew!
DINOS
He's gone... Oh, he lost his hat!
STINKY
NICK

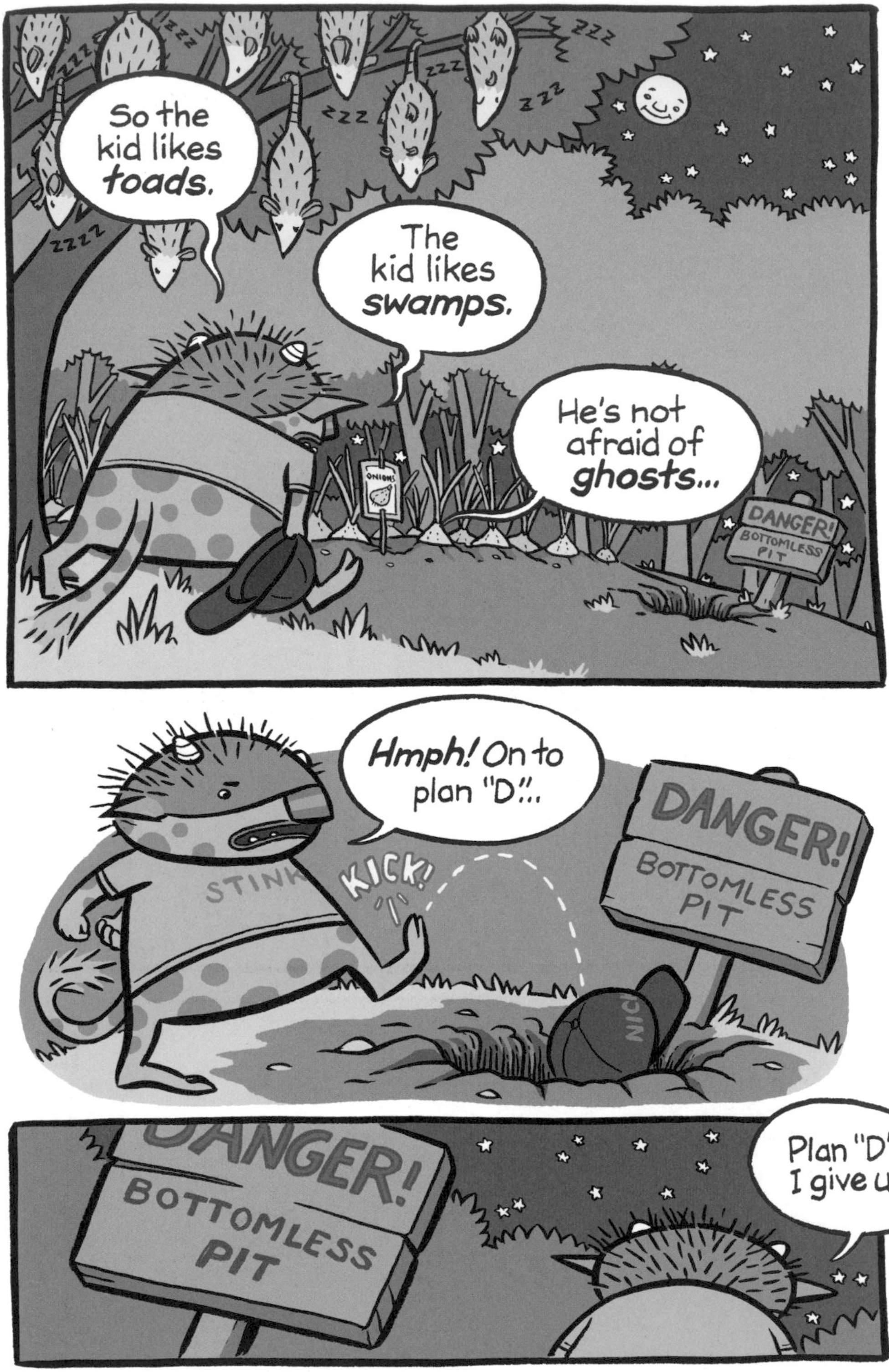
ZZZZ
ZZZ
ZZZ
ZZZ
ZZZ
ZZZZ
So the kid likes toads.
The kid likes swamps.
He's not afraid of ghosts...
ONIONS
DANGER! BOTTOMLESS PIT
Hmph! On to plan "D"...
STINK
KICK!
DANGER! BOTTOMLESS PIT
NICK
DANGER! BOTTOMLESS PIT
Plan "D": I give up.

CHAPTER THREE

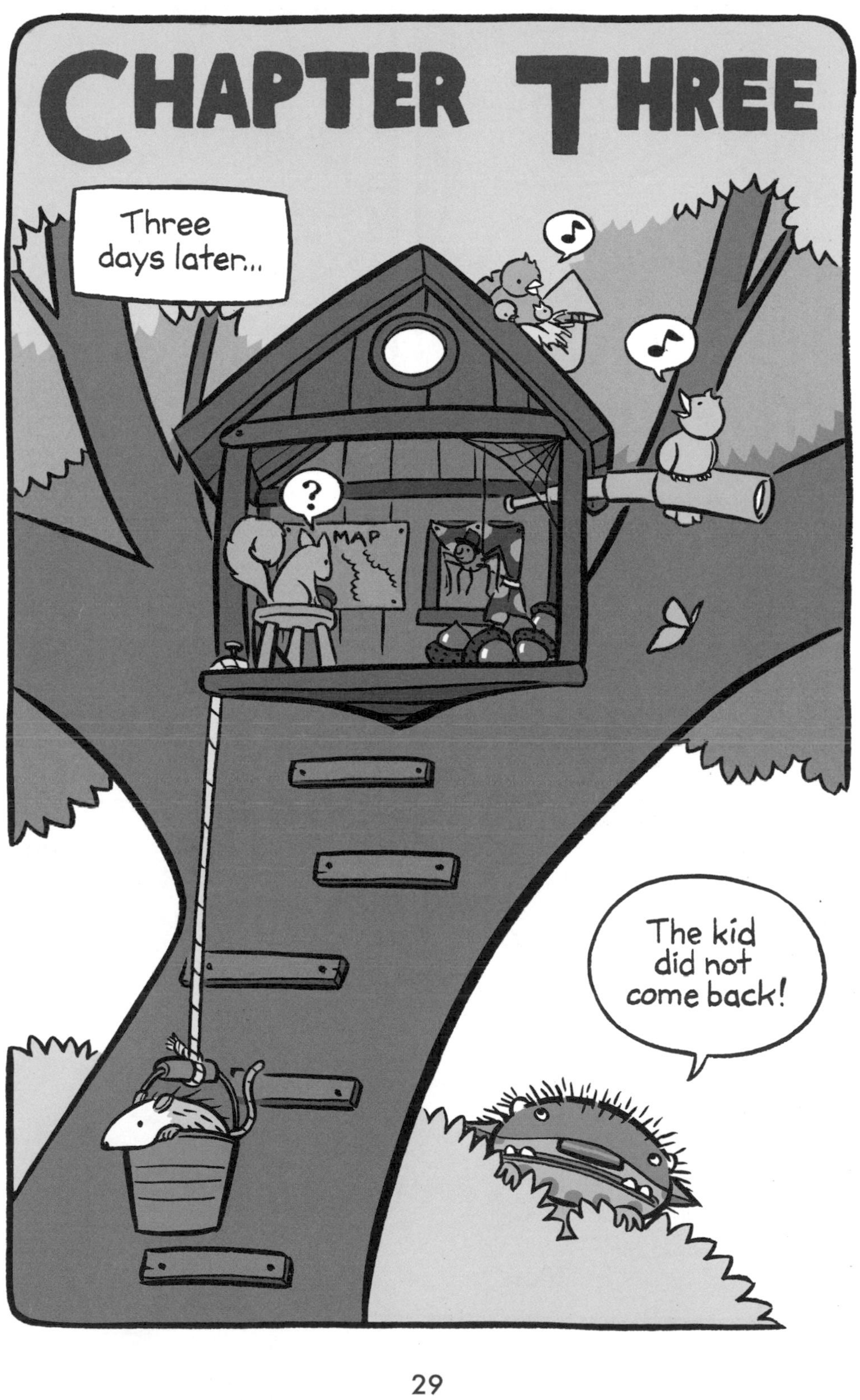

Three days later...
?
MAP
The kid did not come back!

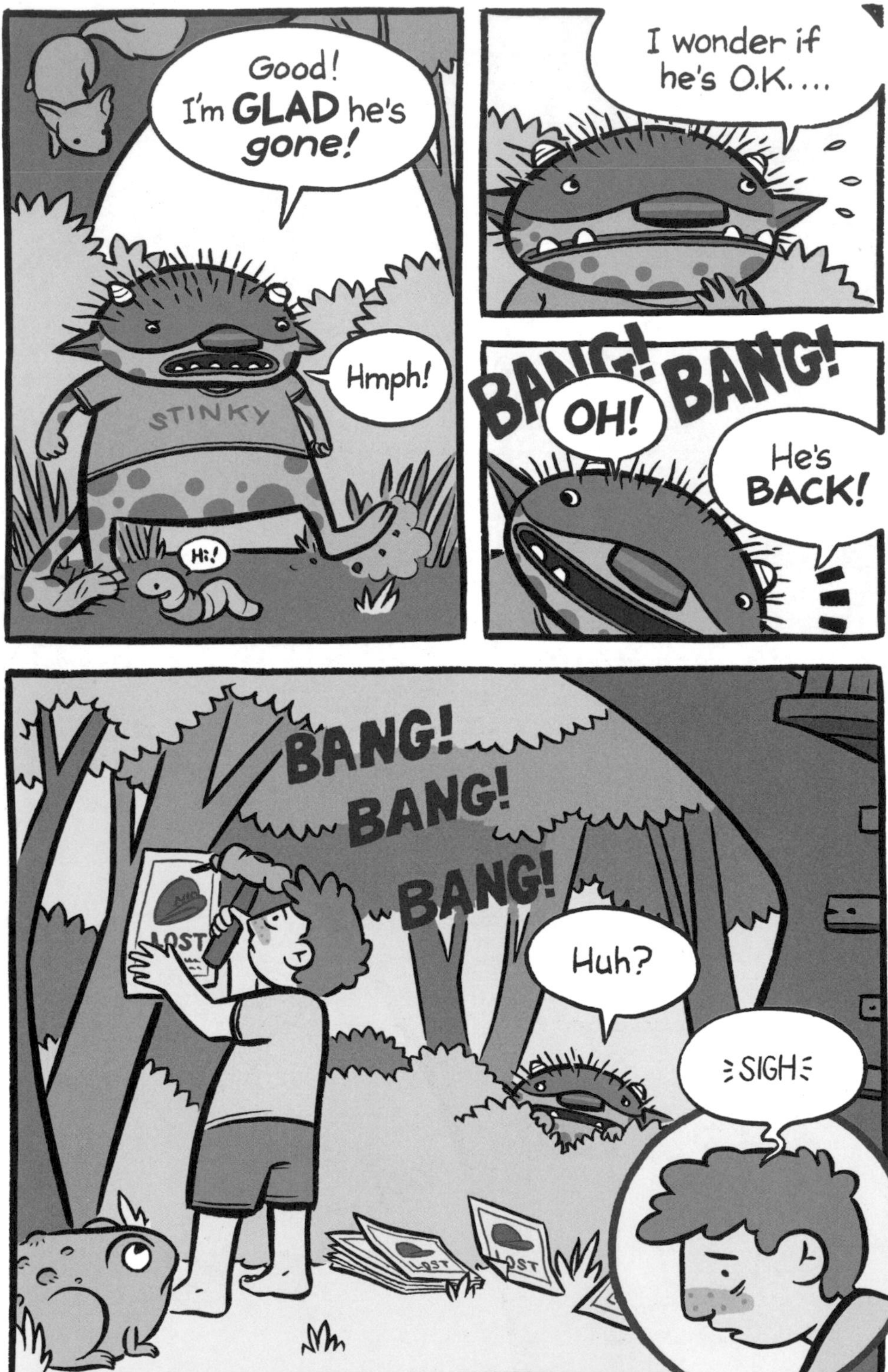
Good! I'm GLAD he's gone!
Hmph!
Hi!
STINKY
I wonder if he's O.K....
BANG! BANG!
OH!
He's BACK!
BANG!
BANG!
BANG!
LOST
Huh?
SIGH

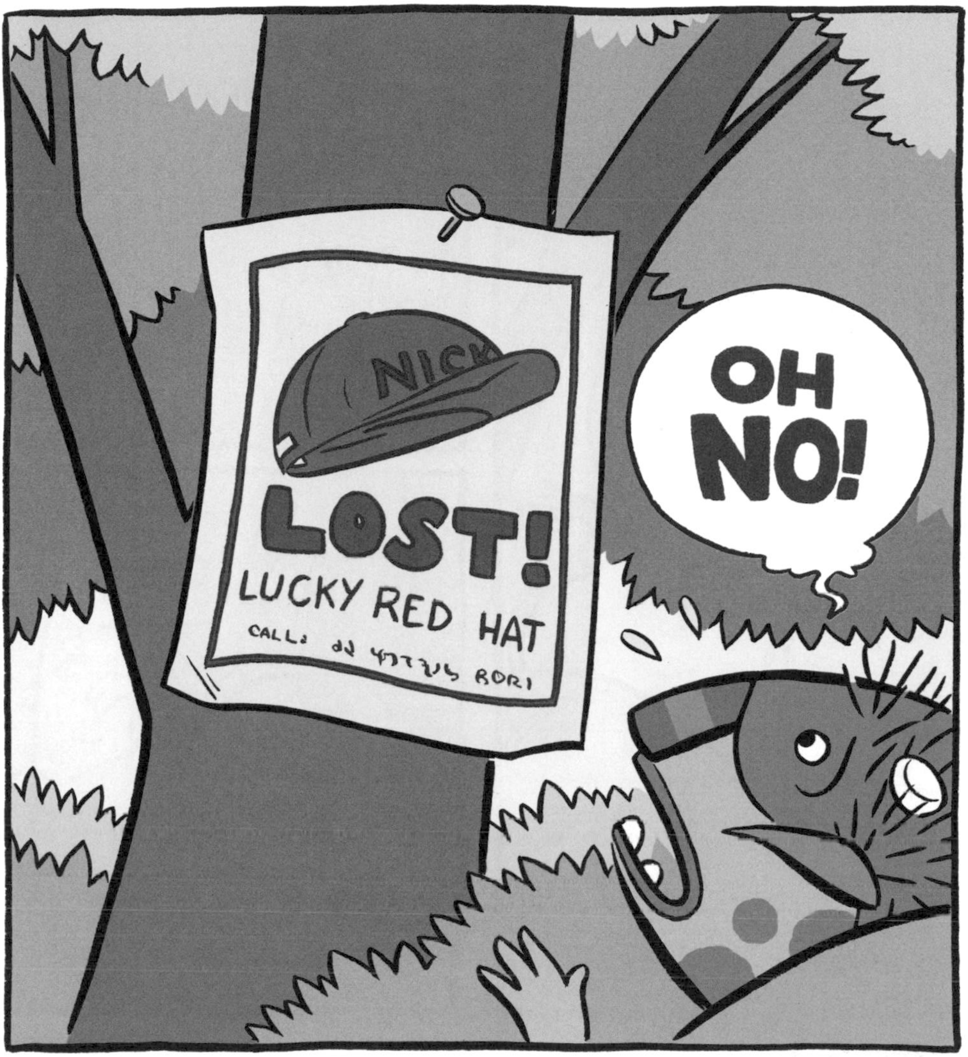
NICK
LOST!
LUCKY RED HAT
OH NO!

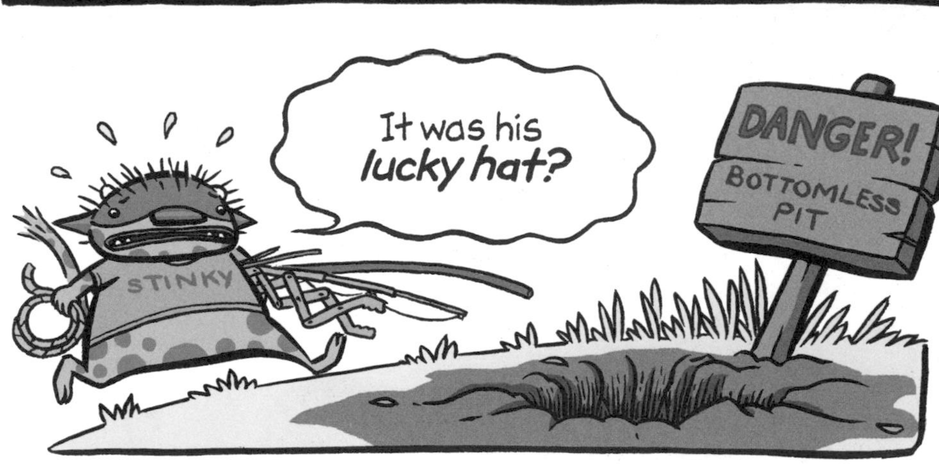
STINKY
It was his *lucky hat?*
DANGER!
BOTTOMLESS PIT

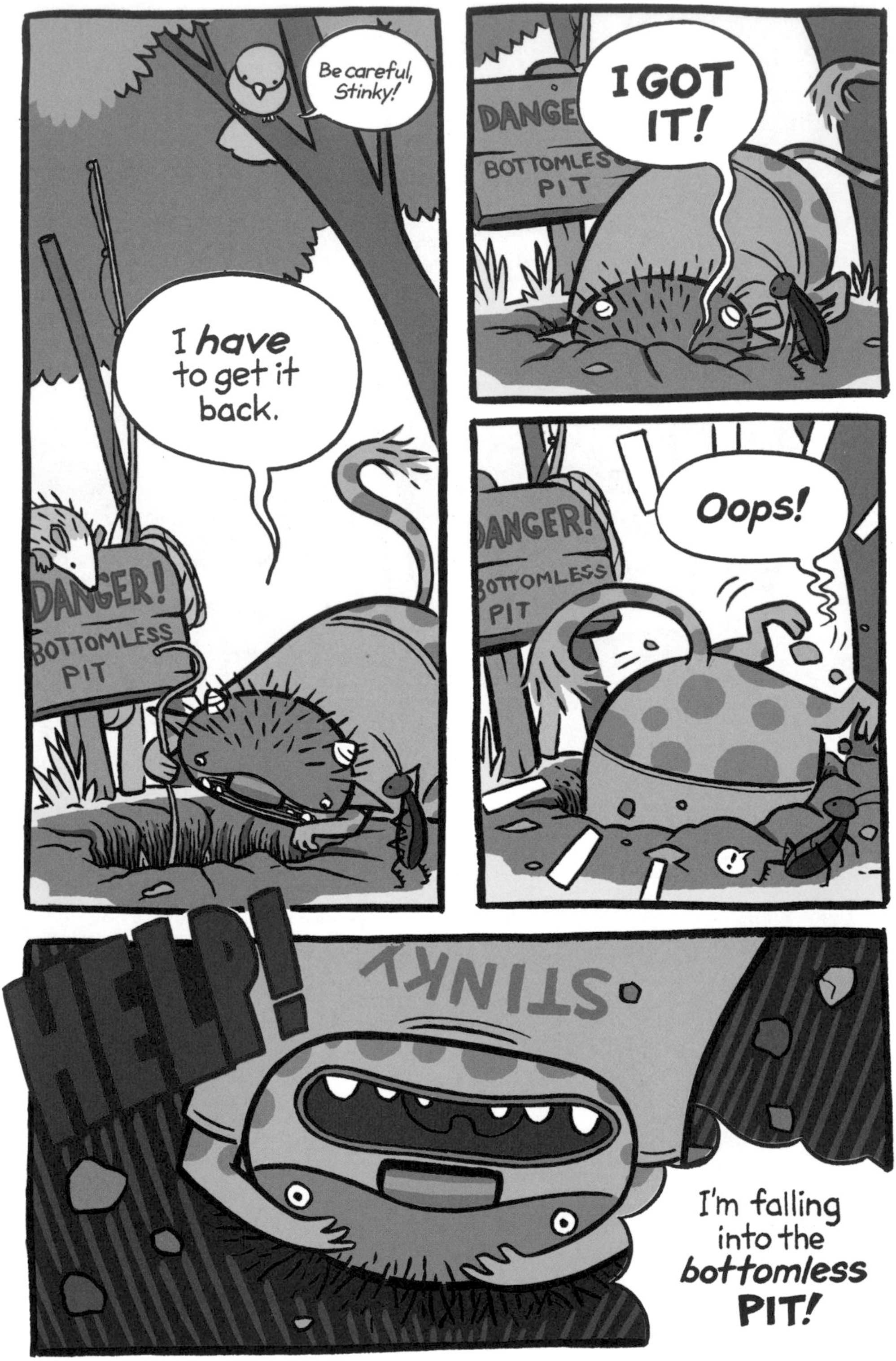

Be careful, Stinky!
I have to get it back.
DANGER! BOTTOMLESS PIT
I GOT IT!
Oops!
HELP!
STINKY
I'm falling into the bottomless PIT!

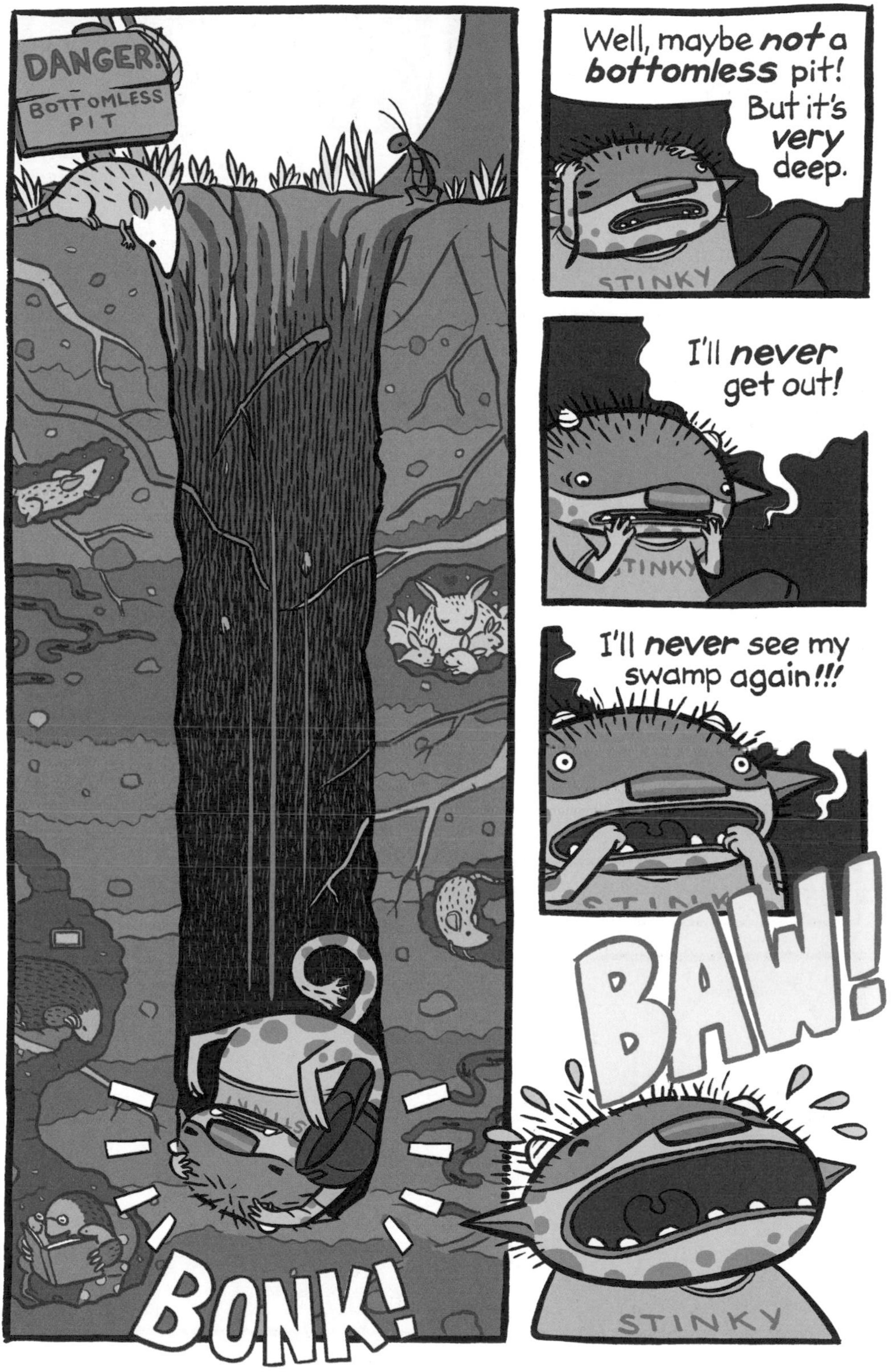
DANGER!
BOTTOMLESS PIT
Well, maybe not a bottomless pit!
But it's very deep.
STINKY
I'll never get out!
STINKY
I'll never see my swamp again!!!
BAW!
STINKY
BONK!

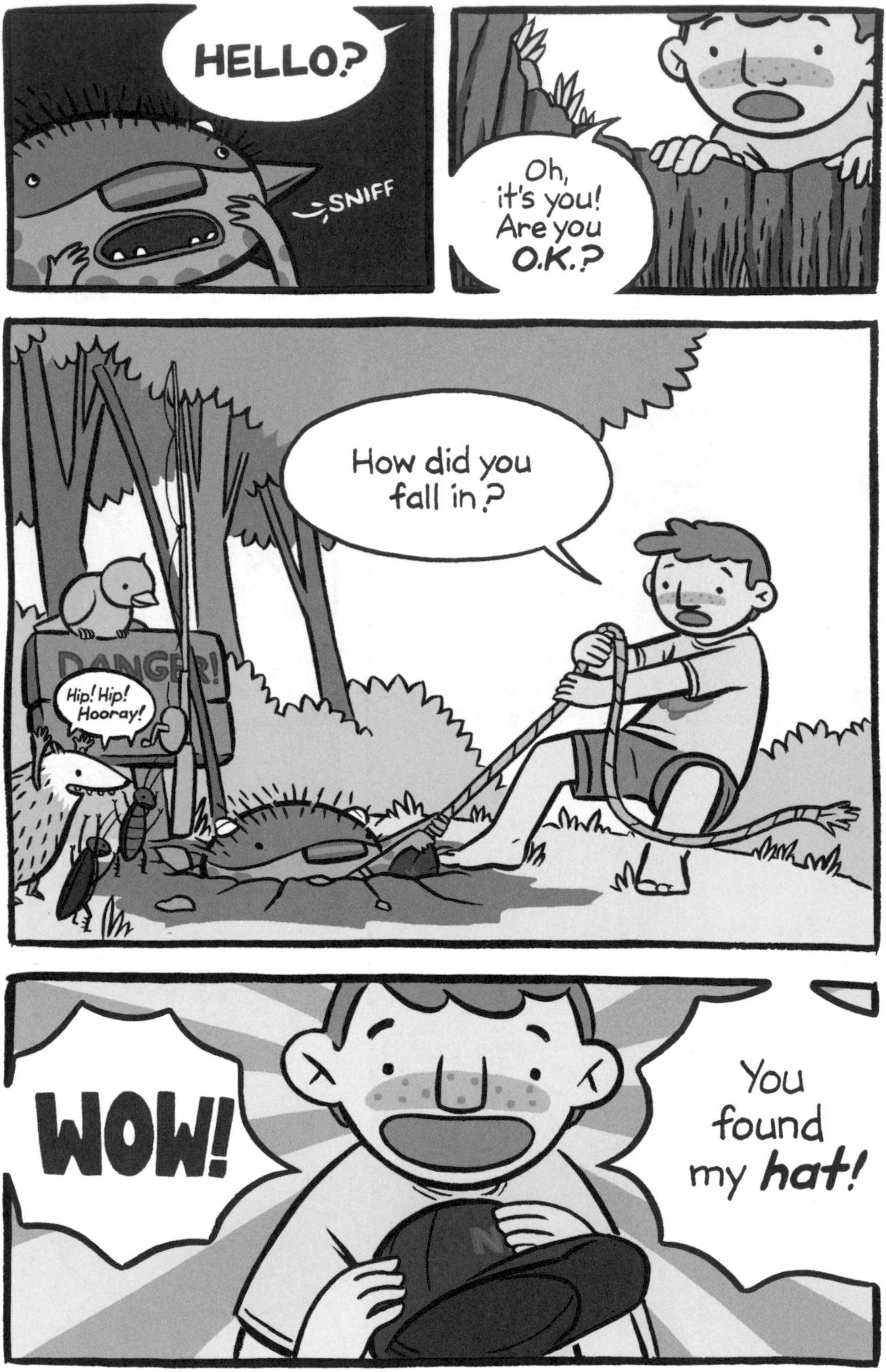
HELLO?
SNIFF
Oh, it's you! Are you O.K.?
How did you fall in?
DANGER!
Hip! Hip! Hooray!
WOW!
You found my *hat!*

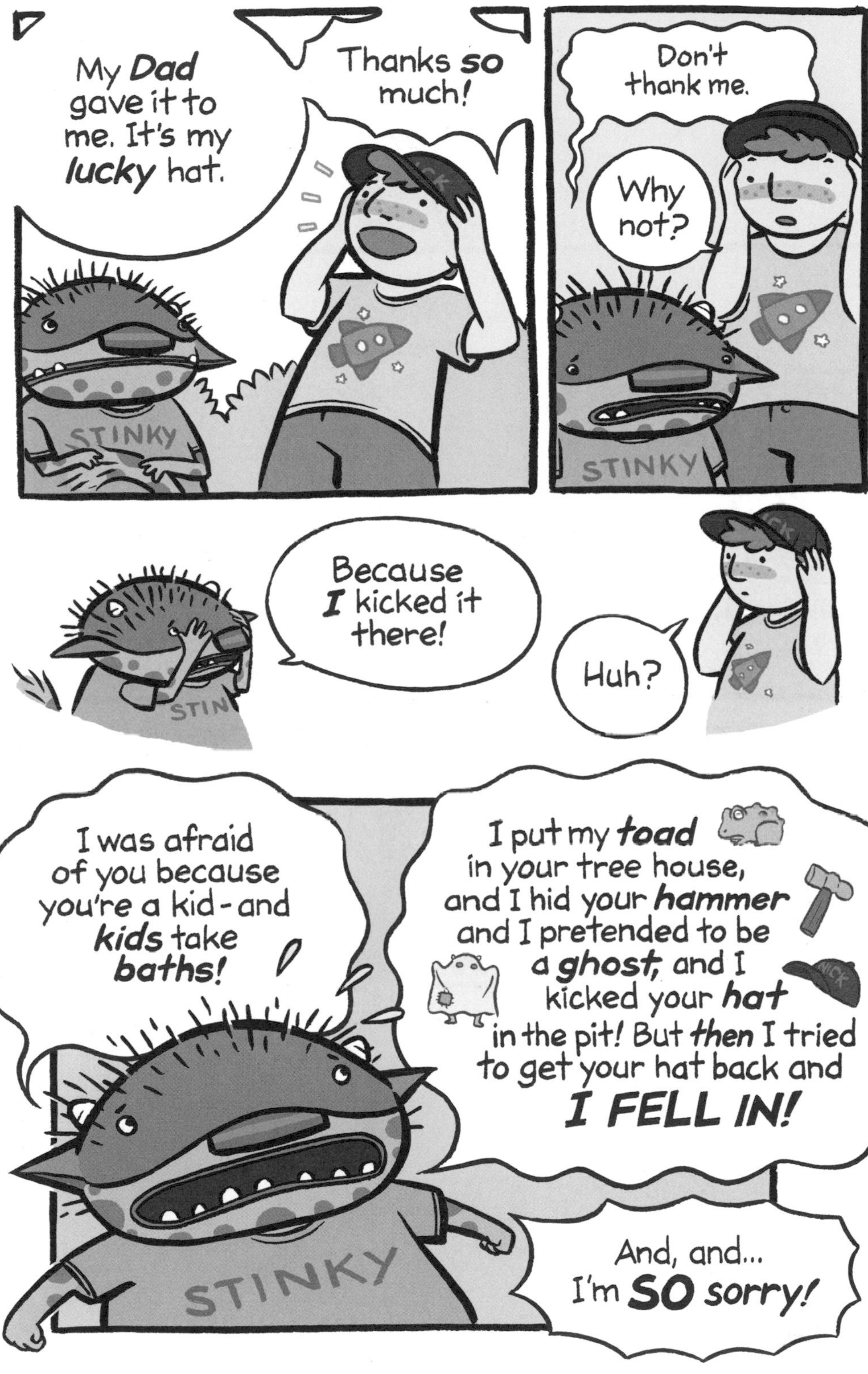

My **Dad** gave it to me. It's my ***lucky*** hat.
Thanks **so** much!
Don't thank me.
Why not?
Because ***I*** kicked it there!
Huh?
I was afraid of you because you're a kid - and ***kids*** take ***baths!***
I put my ***toad*** in your tree house, and I hid your ***hammer*** and I pretended to be a ***ghost,*** and I kicked your ***hat*** in the pit! But ***then*** I tried to get your hat back and ***I FELL IN!***
And, and... I'm **SO** ***sorry!***

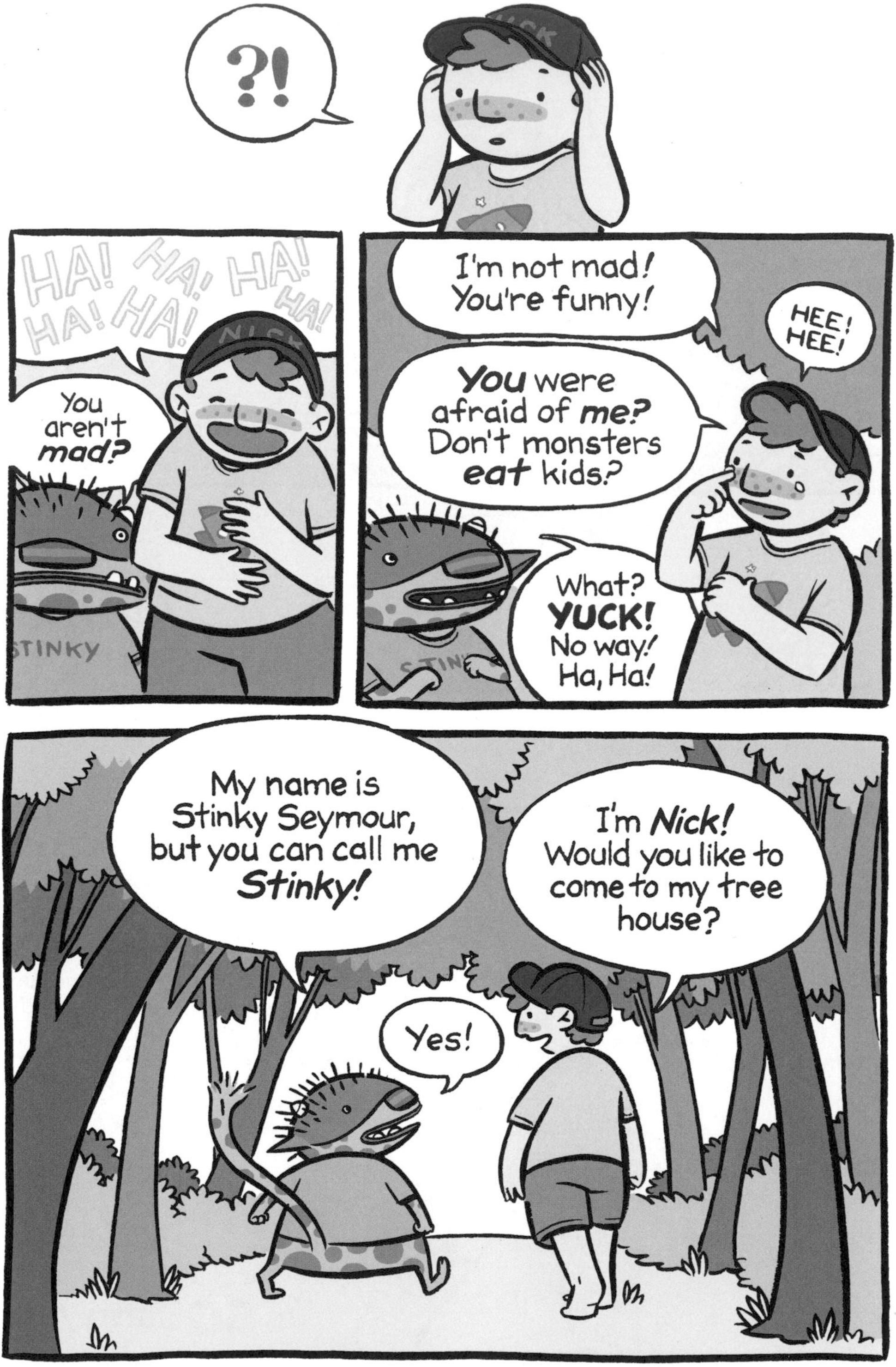
?!
HA! HA! HA! HA! HA! HA!
You aren't *mad?*
I'm not mad! You're funny!
HEE! HEE!
You were afraid of *me?* Don't monsters *eat* kids?
What? **YUCK!** No way! Ha, Ha!
My name is Stinky Seymour, but you can call me *Stinky!*
I'm *Nick!* Would you like to come to my tree house?
Yes!

And then...

Ha! Wartbelly! I *missed* you!

CROAK!

Oh, I see! Daisy is *your* toad?

Yes! But I call her *Wartbelly.*

Let's call her **DAISY WARTBELLY!**

HA HA HA

CROAK!

Would you like an apple?

YUCK!

ER— I mean, thanks!

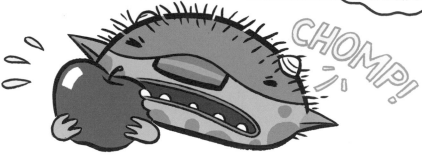

CHOMP!

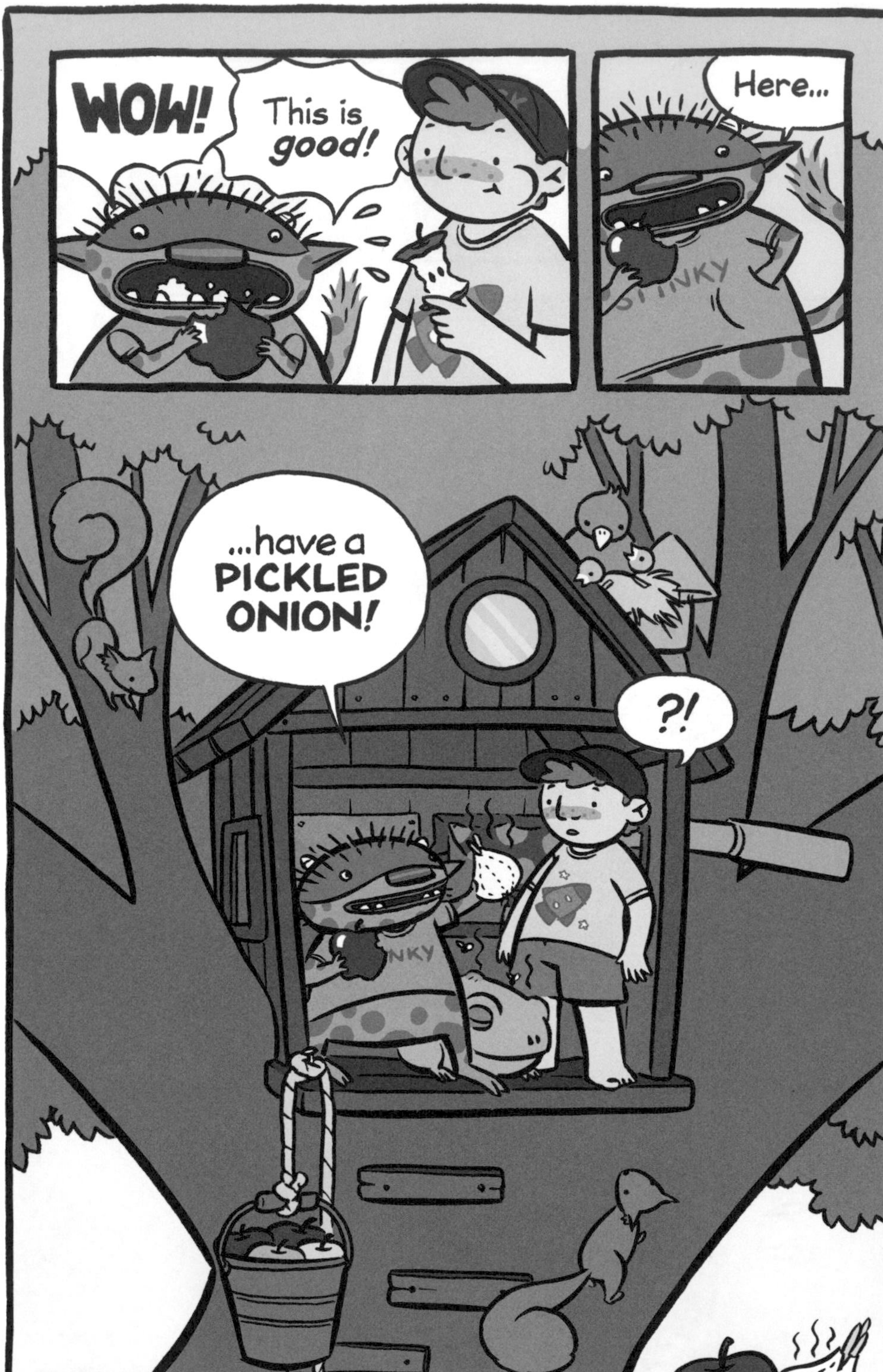
WOW!
This is good!
Here...
...have a PICKLED ONION!
?!
STINKY
THE END!

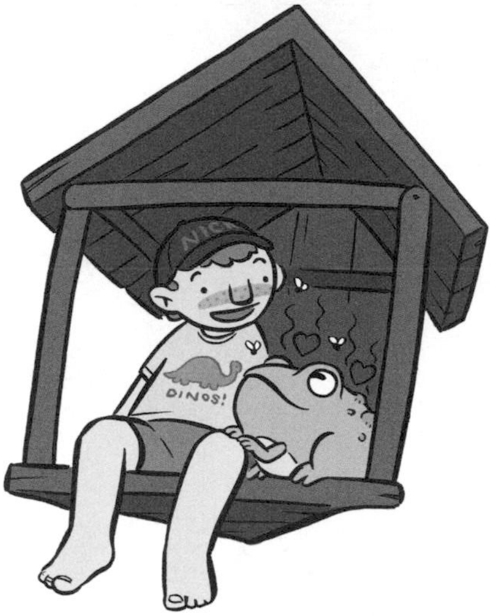
NICK
DINOS!

ABOUT THE AUTHOR

ELEANOR DAVIS grew up in Tucson, Arizona. Instead of going out in the hot sun to play and make friends, she stayed alone in her room, drawing. She started working on *Stinky*, her first published book, while still a student at the Savannah College of Art and Design. *Stinky* earned her many honors including an Eisner Award nomination, and Eleanor was given the Russ Manning Promising Newcomer Award for it. Now Eleanor is widely praised as one of the coolest artists on the new comics scene.

She lives in Athens, Georgia, with her husband (who is also a cartoonist) and three cats (who are not).

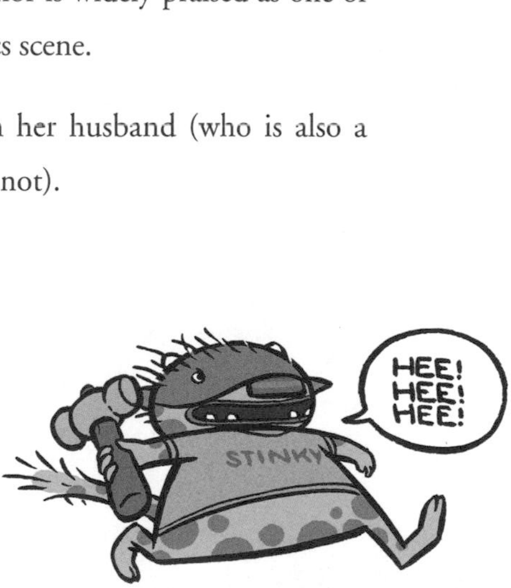
HEE! HEE! HEE!
STINKY

Collect them all...

TOON BOOKS

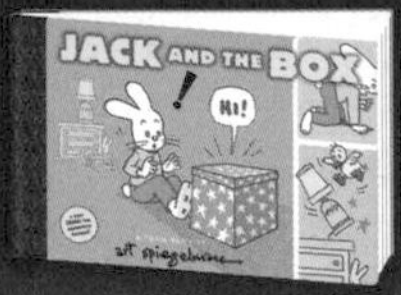
JACK AND THE BOX
HI!

JACK AND THE BOX
BY ART SPIEGELMAN

9×6, 32 PAGES
COLOR HARDCOVER
ISBN-13: 978-0-9799238-3-8
ISBN-10: 0-9799238-3-2

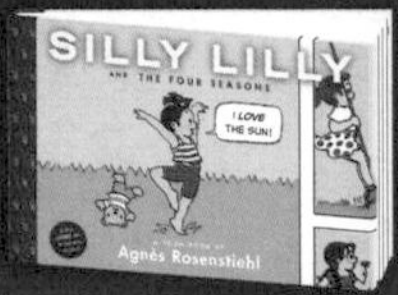
SILLY LILLY
AND THE FOUR SEASONS
I LOVE THE SUN!
Agnès Rosenstiehl

SILLY LILLY
AND THE FOUR SEASONS
BY AGNÈS ROSENSTIEHL

9×6, 36 PAGES
COLOR HARDCOVER
ISBN-13: 978-0-9799238-1-4
ISBN-10: 0-9799238-1-6

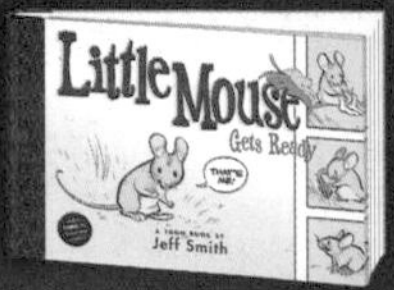
Little Mouse
Gets Ready
Jeff Smith

LITTLE MOUSE GETS READY
BY JEFF SMITH

9×6, 32 PAGES
COLOR HARDCOVER
ISBN-13: 978-1-935179-01-6
ISBN-10: 1-935179-01-2

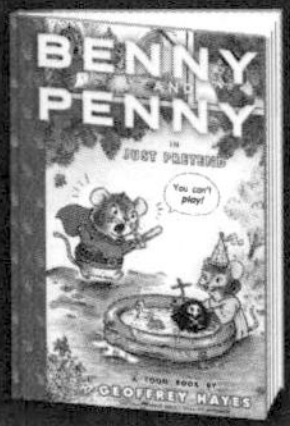
BENNY AND PENNY
IN JUST PRETEND
You can't play!
GEOFFREY HAYES

BENNY AND PENNY
IN JUST PRETEND
BY GEOFFREY HAYES

6×9, 32 PAGES
COLOR HARDCOVER
ISBN-13: 978-0-9799238-0-7
ISBN-10: 0-9799238-0-8

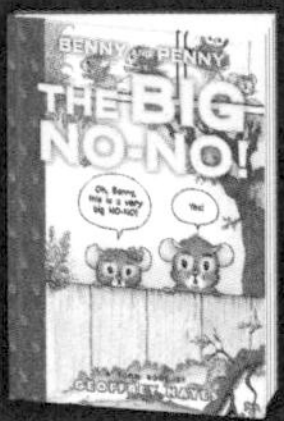
BENNY AND PENNY
THE BIG NO-NO!

BENNY AND PENNY
IN THE BIG NO-NO!
BY GEOFFREY HAYES

6×9, 32 PAGES
COLOR HARDCOVER
ISBN-13: 978-0-9799238-9-0
ISBN-10: 0-9799238-9-1

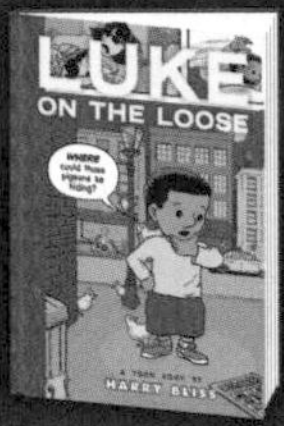
LUKE
ON THE LOOSE
HARRY BLISS

LUKE ON THE LOOSE
BY HARRY BLISS

6×9, 32 PAGES
COLOR HARDCOVER
ISBN-13: 978-1-935179-00-9
ISBN-10: 1-935179-00-4

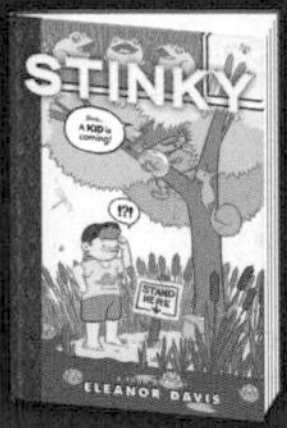
STINKY
ELEANOR DAVIS

STINKY
BY ELEANOR DAVIS

6×9, 40 PAGES
COLOR HARDCOVER
ISBN-13: 978-0-9799238-4-5
ISBN-10: 0-9799238-4-0

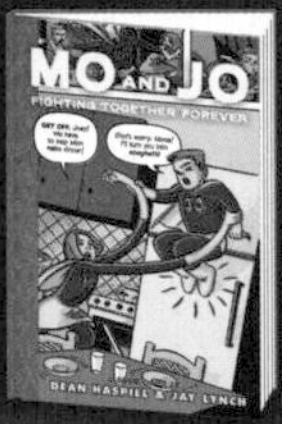
MO AND JO
FIGHTING TOGETHER FOREVER
DEAN HASPIEL & JAY LYNCH

MO AND JO: FIGHTING
TOGETHER FOREVER
BY DEAN HASPIEL
AND JAY LYNCH

6×9, 40 PAGES
COLOR HARDCOVER
ISBN-13: 978-0-9799238-5-2
ISBN-10: 0-9799238-5-9

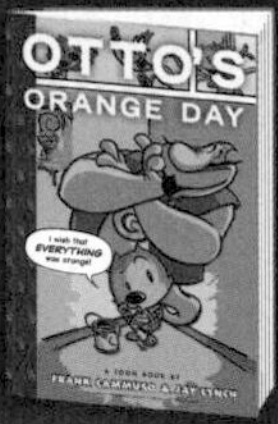
OTTO'S
ORANGE DAY

OTTO'S ORANGE DAY
BY FRANK CAMMUSO
AND JAY LYNCH

6×9, 40 PAGES
COLOR HARDCOVER
ISBN-13: 978-0-9799238-2-1
ISBN-10: 0-9799238-2-4

BRINGING NEW READERS TO THE PLEASURE OF COMICS!